AN ANTHOLOGY

Suffolk Folk

East Anglian Tales
for the 21st Century

Foreword by Costa Short Story
Winner Zoe Gilbert

Suffolk Folk Anthology © 2021
Talking Shop Publications. University of Suffolk.

First edition 2021

Cover design and formatting www.jdsmith-design.com

Published by University of Suffolk

https://www.uos.ac.uk/courses/pg/ma-creative-and-critical-writing

ISBN: 978-1-9989996-0-6

Welcome to our anthology *Suffolk Folk*. In this collection of stories the Creative Writing postgraduates at the University of Suffolk, have taken Suffolk and East Anglian folklore and rewritten these enduring stories as contemporary tales. As an addition to the anthology, we have also included here, the winning and shortlisted entries from the Student New Angle Prize Writing Awards 2021. This award is offered by the Ipswich Institute which runs the New Angle Prize for Literature. Both competitions celebrate writing evoking the rich and varied cultural landscapes of East Anglia.

We would like to thank Jane Dixon Smith for her beautiful cover design and everybody who helped and inspired this collection. Thank you to Kay Saberton for helping to edit the anthology and thank you to BBC Radio and Felixstowe Community Radio for airing these stories, all of which can also be found recorded on our Podcast Show: https://shows.acast.com/suffolk-folk-east-anglian-tales-for-the-21st-century.

Dr Amanda Hodgkinson SFHEA
Course Leader for the MA in Creative
and Critical Writing.

University of Suffolk. 2021.

Foreword by Zoe Gilbert

In Suffolk, we find ourselves beneath big skies. Horizons are far off, and we are open to what feels like infinite air. What could possibly hide, in a place like this?

These stories bring out into the air tales that the casual visitor to Suffolk may well have missed – and may be glad they did, for from them seeps a darkness that the Suffolk sky, on a lovely day, would seem to deny altogether. But even the unnerved visitor will delight in recognising the towns, villages, churches and marshes of Suffolk named here, even if they find them forever changed as a result. Folklore binds us to local landscapes, and the ties here are as insistent as ever. Shiver as you look at the witches' stone in Westleton after you have read 'The Tale of the Devil at St. Peter's Church', or take a moment to contemplate Dobbs' grave in Kesgrave Wood with 'The Tale of John Dobbs' in mind. Remember 'The Faines of Hethersett' when you stumble, bleary-eyed, from a certain pub.

But the writers in this anthology do far more than show us the dark, magical, shadow side of Suffolk. Every piece reminds us that we find deep meaning in folktales precisely because they allow us to see the patterns of meaning in our own, contemporary lives. You will find themes here as new and old as folktales themselves: childlessness, parenthood, loss, destiny, youth, escape, revenge. These writers deploy folklore to help make sense of these experiences, but the lives they describe also illuminate the power of folklore itself. It still speaks to us, and moves us, because we are as human as we ever were. We are reminded how complicated friendship is, and what it means when fates diverge in very different ways by 'Akenham Folktale' and 'The Changeling Who Didn't Want to come Back.' 'Malekin' expresses a similarly powerful message for parents of children who grow up and leave. All our consciences and fears should be pricked by the haunting presence of 'Spring-Heeled Jack'.

Some themes are as ancient as human society, but folklore evolves with us. It may surprise you to find explorations of human trafficking, climate change, ethical consumption and a certain global pandemic in this anthology. But sitting alongside the folktales that inspired them, these stories remind us that some things – human nature, and emotion – never change. Remember 'Eva of Dunwich' as you watch birds soaring over Minsmere; carry the spirit of 'The Fairy Who Died in Captivity' with you and take your litter home. Pause for a moment to reflect on a year of loss when you have read 'The Tale of the Slaughter on the Hill.' And let 'The Orwell Mermaid' serve as a reminder that, however lovely the sky where you are, someone nearby may need your help.

You won't escape deep meaning as you wander among these stories, but you will find humour – another necessity as old as humans and their lore. 'The Rendlesham Mermaid' may be brutal, but she will permit you a wry smile at the follies of incoming city-dwellers to the Suffolk countryside. As for 'The Stowmarket Fairies' – who wouldn't be enchanted by house cleaners who leave tips, the only price being to keep their secret?

As the narrator of this latter story, remarks, 'Linger on that word for a moment: *enchanted*. We Suffolk folk have long considered our cherished county to be enchanting, but let us focus on its essence of the magical, which lies at the heart of this tale.' This invitation serves all these stories well. Approach them with an open mind, an open heart, and let Suffolk and its writers show you what it means to be human, animal, ancient and brand new. You will be enchanted.

Contents

The Original Rendlesham Mermaid Folktale
Retold by Amy Bessent   1
The Rendlesham Mermaid Reimagined:
Rendlesham Rectory by Amy Bessent   2

The Original Tale of the Devil at St. Peter's Church
Retold by Amber Spalding   7
The Devil at St. Peter's Church Reimagined:
The Witching Hour by Amber Spalding   9

The Original Orwell Mermaid Folktale
Retold by Alison Dudeney   14
The Orwell Mermaid Reimagined:
The Runaway by Alison Dudeney   16

The Original Malekin Folktale
Retold by Caroline Roberts   22
Malekin Reimagined: The Gift by Caroline Roberts   24

The Original Akenham Folktale Retold by Carol Love   29
The Akenham Folktale Reimagined:
Raising the Devil by Carol Love   30

The Original Stowmarket Fairies Folktale
Retold by Dinah Cowan   34
The Stowmarket Fairies Reimagined: The Return
of Our Stowmarket Fairies by Dinah Cowan   37

The Original Spring-Heeled Jack Folktale
Retold by Elliot Woods   43
Spring Heeled Jack Re-imagined:
King, Queen, Jack by Elliot Woods   43

The Original Tale of John Dobbs
Retold by Fiona Waters   49
The Tale of John Dobbs Re-imagined:
The Lost Shepherd by Fiona Waters   51

The Original Fairy Who Died in Captivity Folktale
Retold by Hannah Daley   56
The Fairy Who Died in Captivity Re-imagined:
Sara's Strike for Climate by Hannah Daley   58

The Original Suffolk Changeling Folktale
Retold by Hannah King   63
The Changeling Folktale Re-imagined:
The Changeling That Didn't Want To Come Back
by Hannah King   64

The Original Battle of Bloodmoor Hill, Folktale
of Gisleham circa 500 AD by Jeremy Evans   68
Bloodmoor Hill Re-imagined:
The Tale of the Slaughter on the Hill by Jeremy Evans   69

The Original Faines of Hethersett Folktale
Retold by Kay Saberton 74
The Faines of Hethersett Re-imagined:
The Barfly Bumpkin by Kay Saberton 76

The Original Eva of Dunwich Folktale
Retold by Muriel Moore-Smith 80
Eva of Dunwich Re-imagined:
The Wooden Heart by Muriel Moore-Smith 82

Student New Angle Writing Awards Shortlisted and Winning entries 2021
The Singing Tides by Bradley Garnham 86

SNAP Writing Awards 2021 Runner Up, Sarah Clark
Aelfthryth 89

Shortlisted Stories and Poems
Framlingham Castle by Amy Bessent 94
The Afternoon Walk by Jeremy Evans 96
A Good Day's Work in Lavenham by Amber Spalding 98
Christchurch Reminiscence by Elliot Woods 100

Notes on the writers 103

The Original Rendlesham Mermaid Folktale
Retold by Amy Bessent

Down a country road in Rendlesham, a small village near Woodbridge in Suffolk, hidden by the roadside and covered over with thick trees and brambles, there is a pond that sits in waiting. There is great botanical variety there, especially in the summer: primroses, foxgloves, and the occasional orchid are present, but it is mostly peppered with cow parsley. The sandbanks surrounding the pond are high and there are bramble bushes whose roots protrude outwards. It is said that if you pull on these roots, you can conjure the Devil himself in front of your very eyes. However, it is also said that there is something worse than the Devil lurking beneath the waters of the pond.

The pond itself is bent twice into an 'S' shape, like a snake and in its curving lines, the Rendlesham Mermaid is said to reside in its waters. Not much is known about her, but it is said that she pulls children into the waters with her *crome*, an old-fashioned tool that resembles a rake.

Parents used to warn their children of the mermaid, but these days, most people think that the mermaid is just a story, an inventive warning not to play near deep waters.

The Rendlesham Rectory

After a recently particularly catastrophic year, an urban family upped and left their city lifestyle and moved to the countryside. They moved to Rendlesham, buying the old Rectory. Disused for many years, they loved its old-world charm and set about renovating the place with vigour and enthusiasm. When they first arrived, they decided not to make arrangements for things like the internet or the television, so the children Robert and Anne, could learn to live in the country and make do with more traditional ways of keeping themselves occupied.

One glorious spring day, Robert and Anne happened upon the most beautiful scene: canopies of white blossom hung like a blanket above a pond, which was bent out of shape into the slithering curves of an 'S'. It was for this reason that they had lovingly named it the S-pond.

Later in the summer months, they discovered the wild cherry trees were laden with the ripest fruit and after their first visit, Robert and Anne would return home night after night, their lips reddened with the tinge of the cherries.

Their mother would chide them for spoiling their tea, but the gleeful looks on their ruddy faces always suggested that they would only pay heed for one or two days before they would return to sample the delicious fruits.

One evening, they returned home, and the redness of their lips revealed that they had visited the pond once again.

'The locals tell me the mermaid will crome you into the water if you're not careful,' their Mother warned. She had loved hearing this story and thought it delightful that country people kept old myths alive. 'You two must stay well away from the water's edge,' she said, and couldn't help smiling at the story.

'Crome? That isn't even a word,' the children said, in the way that children who don't take their mother's worries seriously speak, full of mockery. They could barely disguise their giggling as they tucked into their dinner: fish and chips, their favourite. Their father had had to drive to the nearest town to get it. But still, that night, as they lay in bed with full tummies, listening to the blackbirds singing in the dark outside their windows, they could not stop thinking about those cherries. They had never known such pleasures of nature in the city.

It had not even been one day before the children stole past the garden gate and climbed up the high sandbanks again. As they did, their eyes were drawn to the protruding roots of the bramble bushes. They had heard an old local legend that pulling on the roots would summon the Devil himself. In this day and age though, the children could not be convinced, and so they spent a while tugging on the exposed wires of the bushes, muddying their hands in the process. When nothing happened, they laughed and continued on their journey.

After arriving at the pond, they were disappointed to discover that they had eaten most of the cherries the day before: the only way to get the remaining ones would be to climb up into the trees. Having been city-dwellers their entire lives, neither one of them was very adept at climbing trees and so it was not long before they gave up.

3

In her attempt at climbing a tree, Anne had got herself stuck in a rather awkward position, leaving her with only one option which was to jump down straight onto the ground. She misjudged her footing, scraping her ankles on the rough bark, yet trying to cling on to the tree all the way down. Where the bark had grazed her skin, it drew blood and started to itch.

'Are you okay, Anne?' Robert asked through a mischievous smile. 'Come on, we'll rinse it off in the water.'

'But Mum told us not to go near it. I'm fine anyway, I'll just wash it when we go home.'

'You're not scared of the mermaid, are you?' Robert taunted, knowing his words would encourage Anne to go to the edge of the pond.

When the light through the trees shimmered on the water like gold, it made the pond clear and exposed the verdant plant-life underneath the surface.

Anne thought that perhaps she would like to catch a glimpse of the mermaid. She might be pretty and kind and she could be her little secret. She paddled in the shallows first of all, slowly becoming more and more comfortable with the increasing depth, even though the water was cooler than it looked.

Robert took his shoes off and dipped his feet in, also enjoying the feeling of the water on his skin. Anne closed her eyes and let the plants tangle loosely around her feet. Their cool touch felt soothing on her grazed skin. Then she suddenly felt something coil itself around her ankle.

'Robert!' she said. He had caught hold of her. 'This isn't funny, Robert!'

She opened her eyes, but Robert was not there.

Water crept around her neck as she flailed her arms around, turning frantically so she could find her brother.

She opened her mouth, but her screams were stifled by the onslaught of water in her throat.

Her eyes stayed wide open when her head became fully submerged, and the last thing she saw was the water-hag's green hand around Robert's arm where she had dragged him under, into a dreamless sleep in her waiting arms.

The Original Tale of the Devil at St. Peter's Church
Retold by Amber Spalding

St. Peter's Church stands in the centre of a vast, Suffolk landscape. As the pivotal landmark in the rural village of Westleton, the church is home to a deadly tale. Built in 1340, St. Peter's Church has been cursed with bad luck. The church's exterior is so unusual that it is bereft of a tower or spine, yet it has a cottage-like thatched roof.

The church can be found by walking along Bowman's Lane, then, by taking a left down Devil's Lane. The name itself brings about its own fears with local families. Mothers conjure stories about a phantom called Blue-nosed Fisk to warn their children of the dangers of wandering off. It is said that he patrols the lane, scaring off any children in sight. Beside the feared Devil's Lane is a dusty track that takes you all the way up to the church.

Legend states that the Devil himself lives beneath the church. It says that if a particular ritual is conducted, Old Nick will rattle his chains below the ground. On the side of the church, sits a 14th century gravestone known as the Witches' Stone. Its deconstructed appearance maintains the legend that grass will never grow over the gravestone. Here is where the ritual begins.

Start on the Witches' Stone and place a handkerchief or a piece of string at the foot of the Devil's door. Next, run around the building seven times anticlockwise. You must resist looking at the door until you end back on the Witches' Stone. The item placed at the door will vanish, if performed correctly. If you fail, you might hear Satan rattling his chains from underneath the church.

The origins of this ghastly tale are unknown. Local legend speculates that Brandeston's Vicar, John Lowes, summoned Satan to help him commit the most heinous crimes. Accused of witchcraft by the Witchfinder General, Vicar Lowes admitted that he had bewitched cattle and caused a ship to sink in Harwich harbour. He was later sentenced to death. Some also believe that the legend was constructed by smugglers who would drag their kegs and bales from Sizewell, hiding them in the nearest safe space – underneath the church, well out of sight.

The local legend still prevails today. Westleton remains renowned for its Devilish sightings at St. Peter's Church. These days very few dare to recreate the ritual in fear of summoning the Devil.

The Witching Hour

I wipe the condensation off the inside of Ollie's car window with my sleeve. It's Halloween. There's five of us crammed in his mini: Ollie, James, Katie, Emily, and me. The heater is working overtime to clear the windows. Looking out of the passenger window, I see the open Suffolk fields. Harvest is over. All that's left is the memory of summer. I check my watch, 15:54. The horizon is hazy as the sun begins its descent. Our destination is unknown to the rest of us, but Ollie is adamant he knows the way.

We take a left down a rugged-looking dirt track. The car dips left and right into the uneven ground, the saucepans clatter in the boot and the sleeping bags rustle underneath my feet.

I tell Ollie that we should turn back but he ignores me.

Emily groans as the car continues to rock. 'I'm going to be sick,' she says.

'Not much longer,' I tell her. A lie. I don't know where we are going, and I don't care. My mind is lost amongst the wilderness.

16:27. The sun dips below the trees and the once pink sky now fades to a deep orange. In the distance stands a lonely church. Its vertical windows capturing the last moments of sunlight.

'Westleton Church,' says Ollie. 'We're here.'

We build a fire on top of a bare stone slab. Ollie says this is the Witches' Stone and we all laugh. We set up the tents and light the campfire. Ollie then invites us all to sit. It was his idea to come, so we let him take the lead. The others open cans of beer. I avoid drinking; I don't want to do something I'll regret later.

Darkness soon falls, so we turn our torches on. The white, artificial light illuminates Ollie's face as he begins to tell us the tale of the Devil at Westleton Church.

'This church was built around 1340,' he says. His eyes lighting up like a child in a toy shop. 'Rumour has it, the Devil lives beneath this church. To summon him, we must perform a ritual.'

Absolute nonsense, I think. Ollie is so full of himself. His shadow follows his every move.

'Starting on the Witches' Stone, we must place a piece of string at the foot of the Devil's door, then run around the church seven times anticlockwise, without looking at the door,' he continues excitedly.

I look at him and roll my eyes. He ignores me and starts to count us down: 'Three, two, one, go!'

At haste, we all run around the church. Ollie and I take the lead, leaving the others staggering behind. I lose sight of Katie and James by lap six. Nearing the end, Ollie and I wait a few minutes for the others to return. Emily runs towards us; her face is flushed. We wait a few minutes. But Katie and James are yet to return.

Using our torches, we circle the building, hoping to find the others. After a while, we return to the campfire empty handed. I hear Emily sniffling behind me. Her torch flickers on the ground. She's crying. I reassure her that Katie and James are just messing with us and she seems to calm slightly for a moment.

I glance at the Devil's door and notice that the piece of string has vanished.

'Why did you take away the string?' I shout at Ollie.

His face turns white. 'I didn't,' he says.

'Stop it,' I snap. 'It's not funny!'

'I want to go home,' Emily sobs.

Ollie agrees, 'Let's find them and leave.'

We search the churchyard for Katie and James. The trees rustle in the wind, it sounds like chatter. Uncertain of what lies ahead, we all hold hands. Our shaky torches illuminate what looks like a rag on the ground.

'Katie's sweatshirt,' Emily cries.

Ollie picks it up. The sweatshirt is stained with blood. Our adrenaline kicks in and we run.

'The car!' I shout.

We climb inside and lock the doors. I turn to look at Emily in the backseat, but there is no sign of her. She has disappeared. It's just me and Ollie left.

'The tale must be real,' I say. 'What have we done?'

'Calm down,' Ollie tells me. 'Emily must have gone to find Katie. We'll just have to wait here.'

21:45. I tremble. The fear in our breath steams the windows of the car. I press against Ollie's warm shoulder and after a short time I feel myself dropping into an unconscious state.

I wake up to cold air blowing in my face. The heaters have stopped working and the windscreen has begun to freeze. I am alone in the car. Ollie has gone.

My mind spins in circles, wondering what I should do. Everything feels so surreal, I don't know what to believe. After a few words of encouragement, I venture into the night in search of my friends.

My torch flickers as I shine it through the trees.

11

Unfamiliar noises pass through my ears, my whole body covered in goosebumps. I run. Suffocated by the thick, black forest, I fall into a pit filled with leaves. As I lay there defeated, my mind races. I think about all of the things I could have done differently tonight. Why didn't we drive away? Why did I agree to come? Only six hours until dawn. I crave those first moments of light.

I hear muffled sounds in the trees behind me. I close my eyes and hold my breath, praying it's an animal nesting for the night. A deer perhaps. I look up into the night sky, the moon shrinks and backs away as if it's frightened too. I hear footsteps. Is it the others? Was this a game all along?

I slowly rise from the pit that looks somewhat like a grave. I scan my surroundings as though I have night vision, hoping to see the familiar faces of my friends. Suddenly, something pierces my skin. A blade zigzags through my ribcage and exits my flesh. The fiery pain quickly turns cold and I collapse into a puddle of what smells like animal faeces. I look up to see a glowing red figure. A bolt of lightning shoots through the sky.

And then, a miracle, there they are. My friends! They are here. I am safe. But I quickly realise that they can't save me. They are also shining red. It drips down their bodies, leaving a puddle of blood at their feet. I must be dreaming. 3:24. The witching hour. My watch has stopped ticking. Everything turns black.

The Original Orwell Mermaid Folktale
Retold by Alison Dudeney

Fishermen avert their eyes,
Few would confess to having seen one,
Believing that mermaids are harbingers of misfortune.

Near Felixstowe, beyond the mouth of the river Orwell, many years ago, a lonely mermaid is watching fishing boats journey out to sea. Quick as an eel she swims with them, falling in love with one of the fishermen.

When the boats return home, the forlorn mermaid is forbidden to follow; for fear of death she cannot leave the sea she was born in.

But still, the mermaid follows the boats upriver to Pin Mill. As she swims, powerful currents jostle her, green riverbanks confuse her. Ebbing strength drags her tail in the water. Unable to go on, she flops, half submerged on the bank near the jetty where the boats tie up, falling into an icy sleep.

Something burning her cheek awakens her. Inches away, the beloved fisherman bares his teeth, strange flat-edged big things. Elated, yet confused, the mermaid opens her mouth displaying her own, pointed, razor-sharp teeth. She hopes to be saved.

The fisherman recoils in shock, pushing her away into the

mud, and for too long after this strange meeting, he dreams of a demon fish-woman. He vows never to go to sea again.

At low tide that night, the Orwell stinks of putrid river-mud. The stench clogs the mermaid's nostrils, drowning her in heartbreak and mud. Hand over hand, hauling herself towards the last thin trickles of water, sliding into brackish pools, she heads for the sea, for home.

The Runaway

Through a cracked, dirty window, Serina watches a white transit-van leaving the alleyway. The engine noise takes her back to the bowels of the boat which brought her here all those months ago. Emerging in the dead of night at the riverside, after days at sea, chained and gagged like an animal. She shivers in her gauzy, transparent clothes, shutting her mind to the squalid house and shameful things she is forced to do in it. He will be here soon. The bittersweet highlight of her miserable days; the boy on the scooter passing by every morning, like clockwork. It is nearly time.

Leather cuffs chafe her ankles and the chains that join them clink as she shuffles to the door. Routinely, she tries the locked door but for once, it opens. They have forgotten to lock it. Surprised, she hobbles quickly out of the room, slides down the stairs on her bottom, gets to the kitchen and throws herself head-first out of the window, rolling onto the scrubby patch of weeds a few feet below.

It's cold outside. She struggles down the yard into the alleyway. She doesn't know which way to go or what to do. The only thing is to get away. She is fifteen years old and wants a life better than this, or no life at all.

And then there he is. The boy on the scooter, on the dot of nine. She waves her arms, knowing how she must look, skimpy clothes, long red hair blowing in the wind; it's another-worldly appearance.

The boy stops. She waddles in tiny, hobbled steps, as if her legs were seamed together.

Balancing his idling Lambretta, gloved hands on the handlebars, the boy is wearing a dark green Parka and looks, to Serina, like a saviour.

'Help me,' she implores him. '*Ajuta-ma*. Please. Take me.'

She points at the scooter. He is staring at the cuffs and chain across her ankles, fear in his face.

'Quickly! Now!'

The boy has confusion written all over his face. She fears he is going to leave her there.

He kicks the footrest of the Lambretta out and offers her his hand. 'I must be mad.' She hears him mutter as she lets him lift her – it is clear she cannot do this unaided – up onto the pillion seat. His hands feel hot against her skin and for once she enjoys the feeling of being held.

'We must go from here now. Now!' she whispers, opening her eyes wide, hoping their deep green beauty will beguile him.

And yes, the boy revs the Lambretta hard and turns back the way he has come, flying them through back-roads, across a corner of town out alongside the full, fast-flowing river. Serina feels a tug on her heart. The river is like an umbilical cord, joining her invisibly to her family. She dares not even hope to go home. Seeing white transit vans at every turn, each of them is an omen for her.

They take a lane near the river, up a wooded drive to an old house. He stops the scooter. She lets him carry her, past the house to a shed at the end of the large garden, almost into the woods. In the shed the boy pulls tools off the walls, a small axe, a pair of wire cutters. Tenderly, he cuts the manacles off the girl's ankles. They don't speak until she is free.

'Thank you.'

She turns her gaze to him, the mesmerising one where she knows the green of her eyes is like a running ocean, one that a man might drown in.

'What's your name?' he asks.

'Serina.'

'I'm Fisk.'

'Fisk,' she tries it out on her tongue.

'It's Swedish for fish. My mother is Swedish. She has a sense of humour. What does Serina mean?'

'Serina means mermaid.'

'You look like a mermaid,' he says. She watches a blush flood his face.

'A mermaid?' She laughs. 'In my country, mermaids are unlucky.'

'That's just folklore,' the boy says. 'Are you hungry, Mermaid?'

He takes her hand and leads her to the house. She relishes the ease of movement without manacles. The only time she has been free of them recently is when they bring a man to her.

In the house the boy offers warm clothes to put on.

'My sister's,' he says, leaving her to dress herself.

He makes coffee and puts out a packet of biscuits. She eats them all, washing them down with hot coffee.

'No,' she says, through mouthfuls of digestive biscuits, when he suggests they call the police. 'I have run from dangerous men.'

'Who?'

'Bad men. I was stolen from my village and brought here in a boat.'

'When my parents come home from work they will know what to do,' Fisk says. 'They will help you.'

Serina is worried.

'It is not safe. I don't want you … involved. These are bad men.'

'You're starving,' he says.

She realises she has eaten all of the biscuits.

'Hungry,' she says. 'Yes.'

'The cupboard is a bit empty here; Mum goes shopping after work on a Thursday. I'll go to the supermarket and get some food. What would you like? Eggs, bacon, a proper fry-up?'

The boy's kindness makes her cry. She is grateful for his concern.

'Yes,' she says. 'But you won't be gone for long? I must hide.' She is edgy now.

He goes to the door. 'I'll be back before you know it.'

Serina goes upstairs to Fisk's room sits for a moment then crawls under the bed, like an eel, sliding into dark shadows of seaweed. She waits.

Later she hears a sound downstairs. The door opening and closing. Fisk is back. Serina silently slides out from under the bed and runs lightly downstairs. Turning into the kitchen, she sees no one. She takes a glass and fills it with cold water from the tap. That's when she realises Fisk has not come back. She freezes. The men have found her.

Strong hands grasp her roughly. She recognises their cruelty; it makes her nauseous. Through the kitchen window, she glimpses a patch of white. It's the van parked in the woods. Seeing both fear and anger in their eyes, it dawns on her that for these men, she is the unlucky mermaid. Her innocence stolen; she holds no special value to them. Keeping her is too great a risk now the boy knows her.

When they have finished with her, they will discard her in the river.

At low-tide the riverbank stinks of wet mud. The stench clogs Serina's nostrils. It's dark like she is submerged in mud. Her hands slip as she hauls her broken self through the sludge towards the dark waters of the Orwell.

She imagines Fisk returning to the house with eggs and bacon and good things to eat. She imagines he is coming to find her down here, where the rising sea covers everything.

But he isn't coming. Her mind is disorientated. He was just a boy and perhaps he will think she has run away from him.

She worries she left the tap running, the water over-flowing the sink, filling the kitchen like a rising tide. If his mother is angry to find the house flooded, he can blame Serina. Blame your unlucky mermaid, she thinks.

She has no idea where she is going, why she is here, in this sea of river-mud. It would be so easy to sleep. She thinks she will swim home.

The Original Malekin Folktale
Retold by Caroline Roberts

This is the tale of Malekin. It is not well known for it happened many long centuries ago.

Some say that on occasion a baby was taken from its parents by fairy folk and spirited away to live in 'another world'.

At Dagworth Manor in Suffolk there came a visitor, a strange spirit who called himself Malekin, who made the Manor his home for many years. Malekin was a bright and clever spirit, but young and incorrigible. He spoke in many languages but always in the voice of a one-year-old child.

Tale tells that the family of Dagworth Manor, a knight and his family, heard a voice in the upper rooms. At first, they were afraid of what they heard, but soon the childish chatter began to engage them, and they warmed to its owner. They began to communicate with the spirit, and Malekin amused them with his funny ways and his tendency to gossip.

Malekin was reluctant to show himself, but allowed the family to see him just once, if they promised not to touch him. He would ask for food often and the family were curious but pleased to find it gone from the special place where he insisted they place it. Malekin told the Knight he had been in his strange world for seven years and that he would remain another seven years before he was free to go back to his own family.

There is a further chapter to this tale. It is said that around three score years ago there was a spirit felt again at Dagworth Manor, which had then become Dagworth Hall. It is said that a man of education was scared from the place by an unknown disturbance that he did not understand.

Perhaps Malekin is still making mischief in Dagworth Hall.

The Gift

I remember the night she came to us. Daniel and I had moved to the Suffolk countryside to get away from our hectic jobs and the painful memories we wanted to leave behind in the city. We found a charming old yellow house as our refuge, surrounded by oak trees and green fields. After so many losses, and at the age we were then, we thought our chance to be parents had passed. It felt as though we had held our breath for so long, and we had resolved to be childless. Maybe what happened in Suffolk was because of this. We had given up you see, on our dreams, and on each other. Perhaps it was that and the breathing out and resigned sighs that brought her to us. Because she at last arrived.

It was a midsummer's eve in our quiet hamlet, our second summer in Suffolk. We could not sleep. The smell of foxglove flowers lingered in the warm air, intoxicating bees that wended their way home through the garden, while moths danced with one another around the porch light. Daniel and I welcomed her together, seeing her for the first time in the soft blue of midnight.

The house was suddenly filled with life, as though a spirited wind had blown in through the open window and woken the dust from its corners. Even in the unloved nursery, up high in the attic where the moon shone bright through its windows. The unnerving cries of life rang through the timbers and shook the spiders from their webs.

She was a gift to us after our grief. Her eyes were the hue of green ferns which brought colour into our dark world which had left us with empty arms and heavy hearts. We hardly believed that she was real. She filled the world with unknowing and made bewildered pioneers of us both. Each day there was a new riddle to solve, and a new curiousness to unravel.

Time shifted into a different realm as, hour by hour, we held her every need in our hands. The waking and walking, the tears and uncertainty, and every creaking step of the winding flight up to the nursery an adversary in our pursuit of her contentment. I recall now the days and nights spent studying her, cradling her to me in the quiet of the nursery. The soft curve of her plump cheek as it rounded into a chin that held aloft sweet lips bowed into a cupid's kiss. She had odd, curling wisps of fair hair that settled around her ears yet nowhere else, and her smooth, unblemished skin still showed beneath it the fibrous veins of her recent making.

The whole house was alive to this welcome interloper, and we learned to soothe her.

Each Harvest moon brought with it her fresh mysteries. The unknown babbling was slowly untangled, note by note, as she schooled us in her idiom; an evolving chatter that we alone interpreted. Each little movement revealed to us her desires, and her bright, blinking eyes studied us just as inquisitively in return. Her peculiar ways became known to us and we learned to love this stranger in our midst. Her laughter was our laughter and her woes our woes. We seemed connected by an invisible thread that strengthened with every grasp of understanding.

She was a companion like no other, making the house her playmate too, leading us to play with her in places we had never yet discerned. Her unbound laughter pealed from every window and across the meadow where at the neighbouring ford, a Robin bathing in its shallow water cocked his head and flitted up to a tree. In the garden, fresh buds on the fuchsias seemed to unfold a little each time they heard the sound.

She held us within her spell, captivating even the pill bugs and beetles that sneaked their way in under the kitchen door. Each fascinated in turn by the tiny hairs on her squirming toes as she lay on the rug. The hazel dormouse slept fast beneath the ground while the low sun sent shafts of infinite dust across the room, warming our backs as we told her tales of faraway lands.

Many Christmases passed, and with each new snow she grew in beauty, strength and grace. We settled into the joy of one another. Peace surrounded us and we continued to trade in stories and fables, eager to believe in them. Still willing to share our thoughts, she began to show us things we didn't know. She taught us how to love and care for her, and how to love each other again, until we thought our hearts would break.

She was always and only herself. She shared with us her gifts; leaving skilful snowflakes on the steamed windowpanes, her delicate fingertips tracing each unique line of symmetry. We would watch through them as the bright frost sent rabbits into their burrows and the barn owl hooted and puffed its feathers against the icy wind.

The old house stood its ground as she expanded into it, seeming to fill every room, right up to the chimney breast where on quiet nights you could hear the crickets chirping. The sound of running feet echoed up and down the benevolent stairs, the weight of ever-growing footprints leaving their mark. The front door shut itself to protect her against the elements, as tiny draughts of chilly air crept their way in around its ancient frame. The inglenook sheltered us on the coldest days and warmed us by a crackling fire, its great oak beam bearing scars from three festive stockings, hung year after year.

More than a dozen Springs had come and gone before she left us. And we knew she would. Nature, as always, had its own way. The enduring little bird box on the oak tree had seen the last of its inhabitants take flight. Daffodils crowded around the old house and bright yellow cowslips nodded their heads as far as our eyes could see.

She was leaving us. It was time.

Slowly the landscape began to change, and the strangeness returned. Time shifted and the world became wild again and we knew we couldn't keep her.

Nothing fitted any more. Words jarred and remained unspoken between us, settling instead upon the dim-eyed moon that gazed back knowingly. Questions were left unanswered, and some we understood were just not ours to ask.

I can never forget how her steady, green eyes looked back at us. We knew she would not be with us long. No magical tales could hold her now and though we clung on with loving hands; clutching at the ebbing moments of calm and connection, the thread between us pulling thinner and thinner.

Slowly, gradually, she started to drift away. The child that we had come to know began to disappear from us, further and further until with one last difficult embrace, we let her go. Magpies cried in sorrowful acknowledgment as the clicking latch on the nursery door sounded hollowly down throughout the house.

And she was gone.

The Original Akenham Folktale
Retold by Carol Love

Akenham Church is part of a small hamlet three miles north of Ipswich. The church is abandoned but under the care of the church conservation trust. It is isolated apart from a farm which backs onto its graveyard. The road to the church is a quarter of a mile away from the nearest thoroughfare.

The church has many rumours of strange happenings. It has been reported that the bells ring for no reason, and a ghost has appeared at its window. It is most known for a legend which has been passed down from generation to generation which says that the Devil slumbers under a split gravestone and you risk his ire by running around the church thirteen times anticlockwise.

Raising the Devil

It was Kai's idea to go and look for the church. The previous weekend Kai's uncle had told him the local legend. When he had been about Kai's age eleven, he and a group of friends had gone up to the church. They had all dared each other to run anticlockwise around the church, thirteen times. He remembered shouting 'Six! Six! Six!' at each lap and afterwards standing at the church's door looking up at its steeple, into the eyes of a lion headed gargoyle that rested there, waiting to see if the Devil himself appeared.

The church as it happened was not too far to walk and Kai had already spent most of that summer in and out of fields, exploring.

'So, did your uncle actually see the Devil?' Sam asked sceptically, as they walked the dusty road up to the church. Sam didn't much like Kai's uncle, he kept a ferret that had bit him once.

'He wasn't sure what he saw,' said Kai. 'But he swears, the Devil offered to grant him a wish.'

Sam followed behind Kai using the soles of his trainers to crunch down on little mounds of earth left in the dirt. He thought Kai was daft listening to his uncle, but he couldn't tell Kai that, his friend idolized him as if he was his father – which was only natural because Kai didn't have a dad. Sam felt sorry for Kai. He didn't have a dad and his mum slept all day.

The church was a lot smaller than Sam had imagined and the grassy ground surrounding it was full of old gravestones. It would be tricky to walk around let alone run. But Kai was not put off and after he and Sam deliberated on which way was anticlockwise, they set off running.

Sam gave up halfway through, trying to dodge gravestones was not worth it and he didn't much like doing anything that Kai's uncle had suggested anyway. He dropped to the ground, leaned on his knees, and waited, watching Kai push himself through the rest of his laps, his face quite red for someone usually described as pasty.

When Kai shouted 'Six! Six! Six!' for the last time, he yelled it until his voice broke hoarse. Sam had never heard anyone make that sound before. It made him feel uncomfortable, as if Sam shouldn't have heard it. As if Kai's desperate sounds were for somebody else, and for something Sam couldn't understand.

Kai stopped at the church's front door, looking up at the lion headed gargoyle. Sam got to his feet, ready to leave, he wasn't going to say anything to Kai about that cry. There was too much in it for Sam who had a mum, who would be sorting out his family's tea and a dad, who would be finishing washing his car right now ready to play monopoly, after tea.

'See the Devil, then?' he said light-heartedly, coming to stand before Kai. But Kai's face was turned up to the sky and the heavens. He was screaming a silent scream, his mouth a black gaping hole that took over his face.

Sam was aware of the silence. Not a tractor, bird or rustling of leaves in the wind could be heard. Terror gripped him. He felt his eyes watering though he wasn't crying, yet a line of water betrayingly ran away from his eye.

He grabbed Kai's arm and shook him, pulling him away from the church, back along the path to the gate forcing his friend to keep pace with him. He didn't stop pulling his stumbling friend behind him until they were far from the church.

Sam chanced a look at his friend to see if he was all right and that he had stopped screaming that awful silent scream. He was relieved to find Kai's mouth had closed but his face still held a look of horror.

Sam tried to get him to speak, to get him to come out of it, but Kai kept quiet, it was as if he was in a trance. Sam walked Kai home and not wanting to leave him on his own, hammered on the door until Kai's mum opened it.

'What happened?' she asked.

But Sam could not exactly put into words what had gone on. He said something about a walk, a church and seeing a gargoyle.

Kai did eventually come round, after Sam had gone home but when Sam saw him again and asked him about it, Kai couldn't make sense of what happened either. The two boys stopped knocking for each other that summer and although they saw one another around school, they didn't hang out anymore.

When Sam was much older, he heard through a friend that they had seen Kai in town, wasted, begging in shop doors, that he had gotten into drugs and was sleeping rough. His friend had said that he talked to Kai and he remembered him, but he couldn't focus on much more than that.

Years went by, with no new sightings of Kai and Sam wondered what had become of his childhood friend. And sometimes, he also wondered if Kai running round that church thirteen times, was the reason his life had turned out so tragic, or if Kai's life had turned out the way it had because of other reasons. But Sam did know one thing and that was if he ever went back to Akenham Church, he would be careful of the laps he still had left to run.

The Original Stowmarket Fairies Folktale
Retold by Dinah Cowan

1st January 1800
Stowmarket, Suffolk.

Dear Parishioners,

As I dip my pen, at the dawn of a new century, and on a day when so many of us reflect on our lives, vowing to make resolutions, I feel the time has come to share with you a tale that first enchanted me as a young child, some forty years ago. Linger on that word for a moment: *enchanted*. We Suffolk folk have long considered our cherished county to be enchanting, but let us focus on its essence of the magical, which lies at the heart of this tale.

George Garnham lived in a cottage on the fringes of Stowmarket with his hardworking widowed mother. They were far from affluent, but his mother was a hardworking, house-proud woman who cared greatly for her son. When she sadly died in 1747, George, still a young man, struggled greatly with his grief and the practicalities of running a house and home. A gentle soul, but infamously regarded as indolent by the locals, he began to fritter away both time and his scant inheritance in the King's Arms, becoming increasingly ragged and unkempt. As you can imagine, the cottage slipped into a sad state of disrepair.

On the first anniversary of his mother's death, George was once again in the tavern, drowning his sorrows in ale and cheap gin. Alice Brown, the young barmaid, eyed him sympathetically, considering what a handsome gentleman he could be if only he smartened himself up. When George awoke the next morning, he was unable to recall how he'd reached his bedchamber. Stumbling downstairs to the parlour, he gazed around, agog. The floor, uncleaned for a year, was swept and polished. A neat stack of wood lay beside the hearth and sunlight streamed through sparkling windows that had hitherto been cloudy with grime.

'I would close that mouth, if I were you!' came a shrill voice.

George started, gawked at the sight of a diminutive man peering up at him, hands on his hips. Clothed in a long green coat, girt about by a golden belt with matching satin shoes, both his hair and complexion were a peculiar sandy hue. As George opened his mouth to speak, an indistinct chorus of childlike giggles rose from behind - he spun sharply, observed in disbelief a hoard of similarly tiny folk scurrying down into the gaps between the floorboards. Swivelling swiftly back, he was dazzled by sparks of fire that appeared to be emanating from beneath his feet.

The little man clicked his fingers impatiently. 'George Garnham,' he pronounced, 'we will be holding our meetings here once a month. But we cannot tolerate mess or dirt, so each week we will clean and tidy. We will leave you wood for the oven and a shilling under the chair leg. But mind now, you ever tell a soul and we will never return.'

And so it was, that every week they came to clean and tidy, and once a month, George would retire to his bedchamber and attempt to slumber through the loud music and chatter of the raucous meeting below. With his home now beautifully kept, George developed newfound self-respect; he sought employment and took greater care in his appearance. Over the years, with his wages and the weekly shilling left by the fairies, he began to prosper. When he proposed marriage to Alice Brown, the barmaid in the King's Arms, she was delighted to accept.

Forced now to renege on his promise to the fairies, George revealed his secret on their wedding night. Far from the shocked or disbelieving reaction he was expecting, Alice squealed with pleasure; how wonderful to not have to clean the cottage herself – and perhaps with the extra income, they could afford a dwelling to accommodate the large family she was hoping for? But alas, the fairies never returned. Mr and Mrs Garnham continued to live in the cottage, and as they were indeed later blessed with eight children, I believe we can hardly blame them for sharing a frequent rueful smile over the disappearance of the cleaning, tidying, fairies.

And so, my dear parishioners, I have so many things to be thankful for as we welcome a new century, but most of all, perchance, the Stowmarket fairies. For if George had not been forced to contemplate his life, and resolve to turn over a new leaf, it is highly unlikely that my mother would have agreed to marry him.

A very Happy New Year to you all.

Yours faithfully,
Rev. Samuel Garnham

The Return of Our Stowmarket Fairies

Since his parents had sold up and moved to Benidorm in 2016 - *the sea air will do my asthma the world of good, lovey,* his mum had asserted, reaching for another Silk Cut - Connor Garnham had been living a rather indolent life. Twenty-four-years-old, and finally forced to let go of the apron strings, he had rented a small cottage on the fringes of Stowmarket. With the cash from occasional labouring topped up nicely by his job-seekers' allowance, he was able to cover the bills, survive mostly on takeaways, and was enough of a regular at the King's Arms to lay claim to his own barstool.

And here it was, that following another humiliating defeat of his beloved team in the local derby match one Saturday, Connor and his mates gathered to bemoan the players' feeble performance and debate the idiocy of the current manager. Their insight increased with each pint, and by the time the bartender rang for last orders, they had also consumed several whisky chasers – each a *last one for the ditch, lads!*

Connor came to the following day at almost noon, fully clothed, with a scratchy memory of the night before and no recollection of arriving home. He kicked out to free his trainers from a strangled pile of duvet, then lay still, fighting nausea and the hammering behind his eyes. Fragments of a nightmare floated and merged. Burglars had held some sort of rave in his house – Stormzy blaring from the speakers, shrieking, banging and all sorts going on. Had someone stared at him from the bedroom doorway? Yes, some weird creature, all dressed up for panto season.

In desperate need of water, he hauled himself upright, weaved across the room and shuffled slowly down the stairs. He stopped sharp at the bottom step. He sniffed. Glanced around, agog. The carpet, usually patterned with fluff and dust and dirty underwear, was hoovered into pristine whorls. In the lounge, the empty pizza boxes and beer bottles had disappeared, as had the smiley face he'd drawn into the dust on the flatscreen TV for a laugh.

'Hello?' he called, tentatively approaching the kitchen, almost hoping to see the growing pile of encrusted plates and tannin-stained mugs, but the worktops were clear and scrubbed and the taps sparkled.

'I would close that mouth, if I were you!' came a shrill voice. 'Wind might change!'

Connor emitted a yelp, glanced down and recoiled. The nightmare: here was the same diminutive man, hands on hips, a green coat swishing at his ankles above gold satin pointed shoes. Up close, he was a rather odd sandy colour, like his liver was playing up. Connor wheeled round and scanned the kitchen for a weapon.

'Don't even think about it, Connor Garnham,' the little man scolded. 'Listen up. We'll be holding our social here once a month. But we ain't putting up with this mess – it was even worse than we'd heard. You should be ashamed of yourself – that bathroom...' he shuddered dramatically. 'Anyhoo, every week we'll be here to clean up. We'll leave you food in the fridge – when was the last time you ate a bleeding vegetable, fella - and a hundred quid on the coffee table. But you breathe a word of this to anyone and that's your lot, mate, we're off. That clear? And go and shower, for

Pete's sake, you stink to high heaven. And you still ain't shut that mouth.'

Connor closed and rubbed his eyes vigorously, was he going mad? Hallucinating? Had his beer had been spiked the night before? Please God, he thought, and it seemed his prayer was answered, for when a second later he opened his eyes, the man was gone.

Connor mulled over this extraordinary encounter for days; he was continually on edge and every time he returned to the house, was nervous of what he might find. Nights were spent huddled under the duvet, eyes wide open, ears cocked for the slightest noise. The ticking of a radiator or creak of a floorboard shivered the hairs at the back of his neck. His mates in the pub teased his distractedness, accused him of being in love. But what could he do? Just wait and see what happened. Probably nothing at all – it was all a mad hallucination - and if it wasn't…oh, come on, as if… but if it wasn't, well, he'd suddenly get the best cleaners in the world who also fed and paid *him*.

But this was no hallucination. The fairies stuck to their side of the bargain. Every Sunday morning, in the small hours, they came and made the place spotless, and once a month, Connor would listen to the music, chatter and laughter begin to rise through his bedroom floor from below, pull a pillow over his head, and eventually drop off. Proud of his newly salubrious surroundings, he took more care in his appearance, decided it was time he earned an honest living, and found work at the local garden centre. Over the next two years, with his wages and the weekly £100 left by the fairies, he began to build up a rather healthy bank balance.

In the summer of 2019, he met the girl of his dreams. Kayleigh was twenty-four, worked in a beauty salon in Stowmarket and rented a flat in the town. She was beautiful, funny and loving; Connor was smitten. But still, although he confided much about his life - how his parents had left him to go and live in Spain – he refrained, of course, from the truth behind the immaculate condition of his cottage and just how he had accrued such a healthy savings account.

Then in early 2020, disaster struck. A viral pandemic was spreading ferociously, and in March, the government demanded all non-essential businesses to close - beauticians and garden centres included. Kayleigh, like Connor, was furloughed at first, but shortly after, her boss declared bankruptcy and she was out of work.

Distraught, in debt and unable to pay the rent on her flat, Connor invited her to move in with him. Kayleigh and her alarming volume of possessions moved in the following Saturday, and that evening saw them cuddled up on the settee watching 'Gogglebox', sharing nachos and a second bottle of Merlot.

Connor, meanwhile, was hardly concentrating on the TV or Kayleigh's chatter. Anxiety coursed through his veins - how on earth could he keep his secret now that they were in lockdown, and weren't allowed to go out or stay elsewhere? He ruminated over the problem until he could delay no longer. Taking a deep breath, he turned the TV up to maximum volume (he remembered Tom Cruise doing something similar in a film when he thought his house bugged), and ignoring Kayleigh's alarmed expression, began to whisper deep into her ear, telling her what he had sworn to never tell. By the time he was finished, Kayleigh was wailing with laughter and wiping mascara-streaked tears from her cheeks.

'You're such a wind up, Con! You and your stories… you're a con, Con!' She thought for a moment then squealed, 'Ha! Con-Con!' With that, she disappeared, still giggling, into the kitchen from where she yelled, 'Could you ask your fairies to stock up on the blinkin' wine?'

The fairies, of course, never returned. Kayleigh deliberated the sudden deterioration of Connor's housekeeping skills, looking at him askance when he squinted at the labels of cleaning products as if trying to decipher code. He seemed a little troubled too, but she figured that was lockdown blues; she was a bit fed up herself.

They are still there, in that little cottage. If you pass by, you may see them pottering in the garden, Kayleigh with one hand protectively on her growing belly. They're doing okay, they're getting by, and while Connor sometimes ponders the dreamlike period when the fairies were in his life, he also recognises that he no longer needs them. He is more grown up, responsible – an all-round nicer lad.

I, for one, am delighted that the fairies came back to the cottage, to help a member of my family once again. I need to watch over my descendants, and young Connor (such odd names people give their children nowadays!) was in dire need of a resolution, just as my George was, so long ago.

Stay safe, dear readers,
Mrs Alice Garnham

The Original Spring-Heeled Jack Folktale
Retold by Elliot Woods

The folktale of Spring-Heeled Jack describes an imp, or demon who looked like a man in a black cloak. They could breathe blue and white flames and had red blazing orbs for eyes, and metal claws for fingers. But the most prominent thing about him was how high he could jump; 9 ft. into the air, which earned him the epithet 'Spring-Heeled'.

He became the typical Suffolk bogeyman who was the shadow lurking in the corner of your eye, or the tapping sound you think you heard. It was told he would target women and would attack them as they walked alone at night. Or he would ring their doorbell and lunge forwards when they answered, slashing at them with his claws. Usually, the tales of Jack were used to scare children into behaving well.

There are supposedly sightings of Jack as early as 1837 and as late as 1904. One tale tells of a man who went looking for a 'strange creature' reported by the mistress of a nearby school. He came across a hunched over figure in the middle of his path. When the man moved around to try and see their face, the figure leapt away into the trees and fled from his sight.

King, Queen, Jack

They call me Spring-Heeled Jack. A charming name if I say so myself, even if a bit unbecoming. Often, they say that I am a thin thing, with limbs that could crack like a whip and bony claw-like fingers covered by black gloves. And that what you would see of me in the night was pitch-black clothing, draped in a matching cloak, that looked like it belonged to a silver-tongued gentleman. It blended perfectly into the shadows, which suited me just fine.

On my head, to hide any evidence of hair, rests a jester's cap in a black and white checker pattern, the two ends curving around like horns over my head. But my favourite part of my description is that my skin is of ghostly white, and the wide smile that stretches across my face, showing my pointed teeth. My smile hides a forked tongue. Orbs of fire are where eyes are not, and a ragged breath or demented laugh causes white flames to lick my lips.

It's all quite flattering. As for the title, well, I hear I could leap up to nine feet and across rooftops. A scary thought, isn't it?

On one particular day, a young man catches my interest. After all, it was quite embarrassing for a person of his age to be banging his head against a wall and screaming like an infant wanting to go home. *Mental health problems*, the teachers whisper to each other. He wanted to leave the moment it struck twelve. Like clockwork, he pulls out all the stops, whining, thrashing and threatening until they are forced to release him back into the world. Utterly powerless to stop him, the teachers let him go, like he is some sort of ugly royalty, like a king.

But I know what he is up to. The moment he flees the people who had tried to help him he will scramble into town to skulk into alleyways and waste the day away on drugs and drink. Mentality did not forgive debauchery, especially if it forsakes those who offered help. It's so obvious, given his mother.

Whilst the King was wasting away, I decided to look up his immediate family, and came upon their residence. No father in sight, but a mother there certainly was. Some would call it quite the grand house, I instead prefer to call it a castle for a ruthless tyrant. A car is parked outside which she clearly never uses to pick up or drop off her son.

The pictures she shamelessly posts on social media depict a woman fat on life with no ounce of work to her name and a small unearned fortune beneath her. She definitely thought herself a queen, above all others with her castle and wealth, the peasants bending their knees and offering up their own hard-earned gold so that she may do nothing to repay them. All hers because of her poor king, off galivanting with gangs. A fat parasite is what she is, sucking all the value from her son and those around her.

She provided all the motivation I needed.

That evening, in my own eagerness, I go to their house and hide outside in the shrubbery. The King had stumbled in not too long ago, his dulled senses making it all too easy for me. Soon after, the queen returns to her castle looking quite unbecoming, perhaps one too many drinks, and goes inside. Now, all there was to do was wait for the comfort of night.

In times of old, tyrants would rule and take what they wanted, but at least they were bound to royal blood. Now, they were everywhere. More appearing each day, wailing for money, so as to gain from the working class and give nothing in return save from sob stories. At least the rich have the decency to play jester and perform for the rest of us. But the Kings and Queens who believe they conquered a system rather than land, are nothing more than fools that mere mortals cannot touch because of their own paranoia. We know what they've done, and I, Spring-heeled Jack, know what they deserve.

The night is dark thanks to a weak winter moon, allowing me to emerge, and walk to the front of the castle. Leaping nine feet into the window was an impressive thought, but a locked window with no means to lockpick would be too noisy. A direct approach would be best. In order to topple this monarchy, I will try the old act of a peasant knocking at the door. Then, when the Queen or King answers, I will grab them by their bloated throat and strangle them until they are dead. The other one wouldn't get far with their lazy legs, and a knife on my person would cease any struggling.

I reach a gloved hand for the doorbell. A scream sounds behind me. I flinch and look over my shoulder through the darkness behind me. A woman, one of the teachers, has pulled up outside the house. Perhaps some misplaced conscience forcing her to attend to the King. She points a shaking finger at me. With stealth no longer with me, I have no choice but to shamefully flee into the night.

Alas, my mission was an utter failure, but a good lesson; a more psychological, online approach was necessary.

I cannot help but wonder if that woman ever regrets stopping me, knowing that the Queen will continue to exploit her son and the system for monetary gain. I'm sure she will on tough days, when she is struggling to make ends meet.

Anybody with the right mindset can do something awful. Imps and demons most assuredly exist today, we're just far more human. After all, we can all wear black. Our eyes can turn red in a camera flash, and our breath on a cold night can look like white fire. You too can train to climb a wall with such speed it looks like you leapt it. Spring-Heeled Jacks most surely exist, they just need a King or Queen, and the right kind of demented mind.

The Original Tale of John Dobbs
Retold by Fiona Waters

In Kesgrave, Suffolk you will find the grave of John Dobbs. The solitary headstone, surrounded by iron railings, sits on a lonely grassy area next to Kesgrave Wood. It is said that anyone who disturbs his resting place will be chased away by his angry and bitter ghost.

John Dobbs, a Suffolk shepherd, led a life full of loss and sadness. The young man had first lost his wife, and then his two baby sons to the plague. With only his sheep for company, John mourned for his buried loved ones. In a moment of grief, he lost sight of his favourite animal, a sheep which another shepherd had trusted him to care for. Heartbroken, John wandered the fields for days in the hopes that he would find the lost animal, but he never did.

Other shepherds turned upon John, accusing him of secretly selling the sheep and keeping all of the money for himself. The young shepherd began to feel more alone than ever. He feared that if found guilty, he would be deported to a faraway land. The thought of leaving the resting place of his wife and sons filled him with hopelessness and despair. John saw no future for himself but one of sadness. So, in the middle of the night, the shepherd hanged himself from the beam of a barn. Fulfilling his wish to be gone from this cruel world forever.

When poor John was found the following morning, the

people of the parish damned the shepherd for committing the great sin of suicide. The local priest refused to bury him in the churchyard next to his family where John had prayed his final resting place would be. Instead, he was buried alone. His body hastily put in a shallow grave at the exact point in the land where the boundaries of four parishes met.

It was believed that placed at a crossroads, John's sinful soul would never find the way to either heaven or hell, instead languishing in purgatory forever.

The Lost Shepherd

It had been a bright but chilly day the morning that the little boy was lost. For Jack, the day had begun like every other. He parked his motorbike at the entrance to the farm, then went straight to feed the sheep and muck out the ponies. Once his tasks were done, Jack then opened the gate for the day's visitors.

Jack was known for arriving early and staying late at the farm park, a pattern which was attributed to his dedication to the farm and his love for the animals. But it was much more than that. Spending his days volunteering took Jack away from the silent four walls of his flat and out into the openness of the outdoors. There, the newborn lambs would bound over to him, and the horses would lean into his side as Jack sneakily fed them biscuits from the pocket of his coat. The animals made Jack feel loved and needed. He knew each of their individual quirks and habits as if they were his family.

It was on this day that ten little boys and girls had walked through the farm gates. They waddled in two by two, chatting away and pointing excitedly at the variety of furry creatures that the farm park's muddy trail would take them to as their teacher hurried them along the path. Jack showed the children the way, stopping at each pen, stable, and hutch to tell the little visitors what every animal had had to eat that morning, and of the cheeky things each pig, sheep or rabbit would do to get his attention at feeding time.

As they reached the farthest part of the farm, Jack showed the children how to feed the lambs and smiled as they giggled at the woolly wriggling animals. As one little boy with auburn hair and a red coat scratched a lamb between the ears, Jack wondered whether his own son would have looked like him. He tried not to think about it too much, but sometimes his mind would wander back to that day all those years ago. The day that had been his son's first and last. At those times, he would catch himself thinking of what might have been.

Realizing that he was once again lost in thoughts and memories, Jack looked about him and saw that the children had run off towards the final part of the trail. He jogged to catch up with them. Expecting to find the children lively and chatting, he was concerned to see a little girl looking confused and upset, wiping a tear away with the sleeve of her coat as he approached her.

'I don't know where he's gone,' she said. 'He was holding my hand but then he ran off and I don't know where he went.'

Confused, Jack looked around the group, hastily counting and re-counting the huddle of children standing at the entrance to the forest. There were ten before, but now there were only nine. The missing child was the little boy with the auburn hair. The boy that he thought could maybe, in another life, have been his own.

At first the search had been calm. The children skipped about the grass looking for the little boy, calling out his name and chasing each other as if it were a game of hide and seek. But then, slowly but surely, a sense of dread fell upon Jack, the teacher, and finally the rest of the children. The jovial rustling behind the bushes, and peeking behind the stables became desperate yells, and frenzied dashes around the land as the seconds turned into minutes. The little boy was nowhere. Jack called the police. The teacher spoke in rushed, hushed tones down her phone first to the school, and then the boy's parents. Jack continued to search. The minutes tuned into hours, and the little boy was still not found.

As the hours turned into days, Jack spiralled into a nightmare. The silence of his flat was broken by hammering at the door by the press, and then the police. The farm, once the only place for Jack's solitary soul to feel alive and free, had suddenly become a place of loss and sadness. The little boy was still not found. When Jack went out, he would think he saw a flash of auburn hair turning into the next aisle of the supermarket. As he walked home, he would think a blur of a red coat could be seen as a car flashed past him.

The boy was never found. Jack did not go back to the farm. He did not go anywhere. He sat alone in his room, staring at the picture frame next to his bed. His own lost little boy. The tiny handprints in blue paint so hard and cold compared to the soft warm baby he and his wife had meant to take home. The baby he had said would be alright when his wife had not been so sure. The little boy who was lost before he had even been born.

Jack sat alone for many days which turned into weeks, feeling immense guilt, emptiness, and then guilt again. Like a shepherd who had lost his sheep. Jack neither slept nor ate. He was fearful to go out again into the sad world as he descended into a state of existing but not living.

When he decided he could bear no more, the young man left his flat for the first time in months. He pulled himself onto his motorbike, his helmet placed carefully in front of the door and drove off into the night. He felt little as he went swiftly along the road. Jack did not stop himself as the motorbike pulled him faster and faster towards the crossroads up ahead. The last thing Jack knew he was flying. Flying away from the earth and into the sky above.

The Original Fairy Who Died in Captivity Folktale
Retold by Hannah Daley

You may have heard the tale of the fairy who was stolen in the dead of night. But, as is the way of magical stories, it must be told again.

A farmer, who lived near Bury St. Edmunds, had noticed that someone was stealing his wheat. Enraged, for he thought it was his competitor, he set a trap for the thief. He hid amongst the hay bales and waited until the moon had risen and owls hooted in the night.

To his surprise, he did not see the neighbouring farmer. Instead, before his eyes was a herd of fairies. They had skin that glistened silver in the moonlight. It was as if they were covered in crystals. Their little voices chimed and cheered as they danced around the barn. They were as industrious as they were beguiling. Soon, they had removed one eighth of the wheat from the barn.

The farmer moved from his hiding spot to find the smallest fairy of the herd in his path. She was dainty and beautiful, struggling to carry one ear of wheat from the barn. Furious, the farmer seized his chance. For who would believe that the thief was a fairy? He scooped up the little creature and stuffed her under his hat.

Wriggling and squirming desperately she cried out, 'Brother Mike! Brother Mike!' to no avail and she was taken into the farmer's house.

The next day, the farmer's children were overjoyed to have a fairy to play with. But all was not well. For, as you well know, to remove a fairy from their magical lands is to doom them to a slow and painful death, as their magic seeps away and leaves them as an empty husk. The children soon grew bored of playing with the tiny fairy and she was left, forgotten on a shelf. Later, when they discovered her dead, the children's hearts were filled with sorrow and regret.

So, if you see a fairy, you must resist temptation and leave them be. For some things in this world are not for us to possess. Some things exist to exist, and that is the way it must be.

Sara's Strike for Climate

Sara took a steadying breath, straightened her school cardigan and walked into the kitchen. Immediately, her nostrils were accosted by the smells of a fry up. Mike, her brother, was hunched over a plate of food, eating with the kind of vigour of that befitting a teenage boy. Sara pointedly turned away and saw her father sat at the table, a newspaper in one hand and a cup of tea in the other.

'You see this? That heatwave has killed crops across the county. They say the wheat and barley has been affected worse. Sad time to be a farmer.'

Her mother nodded solemnly and cracked an egg into the frying pan. Sara walked past the table to the fridge and poured herself a glass of orange juice. She replaced the carton with more force than she intended, and her mother tutted.

'What did the carton do to you?' said her father laughing as Sara's mum slapped down a plate of bacon, sausages, and eggs in front of him.

'Mum,' said Sara. 'Please don't cook any for me.'

'Whyever not?'

'I've decided to become a vegan.'

'Jesus Christ, Sara!' her father bellowed. 'I ain't having none of that poncy avocado on toast in this house.'

'I didn't ask for avocados. Did I, Dad?'

Sara's mother then joined in. 'Don't speak to your father like that, young lady!'

Sara ignored her. 'The heatwave you were talking about, that's caused by us killing animals and stealing babies from their mothers. It's all because of us interfering in things that don't concern us.'

'But you got to eat meat for protein, innit?' her brother joined in.

'I'll get it from other things. Like plants, Mike. Which is how the animals get it anyway.'

'Well, I ain't wasting money on that vegan shit when we have perfectly good food here!' her father said, indicating his knife at his plate.

'It's 'cause she wants to go to London with all the other hippy nerds, innit?' Mike added, enjoying stirring up trouble for his sister.

'You ain't going to that today, missy. You are going to school, you hear me?' her father warned, pointing his eggy knife at her.

'Fine!' Sara replied. She stalked out of the kitchen, trying not to cry until she was out of the house.

Sara stayed on the bus past her stop. Whilst checking her bag for her headphones, she looked over the provisions she had packed for her day of rebellion. She wasn't going to school today. Walking along the Ipswich Waterfront, with a podcast playing in her ears she tried to ignore the rising anger that her father had left in her. She sat down on a bench and stared out at the boats moored on the river.

It was a still calm day. The sun beating down in a cloudless sky, but the heatwave did seem to be ending. Upon the surface of the water, a swan made its way through the green algae leaving a snail-trail of clean water in its wake. She was going to start university soon. Surely, she should be the one to decide what she did or didn't eat? It wasn't as though she'd walked into the kitchen and announced that she was on drugs or pregnant. Some parents had it worse than their child wanting to save the planet. Why couldn't they be proud of her? Join her even?

As Sara sat there, she noticed that the water wasn't just home to boats, algae, and swans. The green algae was interspersed with empty plastic bottles, crisp packets, and beer cans. After a short while, she watched a young man chuck his cigarette stub into the water. He didn't spare the river a second glance as he continued on his way. The cigarette laid on the algae, still smoking.

Sara wanted to leap at the man. Yell and scream at him that *he* was the problem. That his lack of respect for the river had contributed to the heatwave and its devastation on crops and wildlife. She wanted to strike the man, claw at his face with her silver nails and send him hurling into the river to see how he liked it. But she didn't. Instead, Sara scowled at the man as he walked past her.

Right now, in London, people would be crowding the streets striking for the climate emergency. Sara wished she was with them. Her parents had refused to let her miss school to go to London and join the protest. So, she set up a protest of her own.

She could still strike right here, right now in Suffolk. On her bench that she would not move from until the end of the school day. She had packed herself some water and snacks. She wasn't moving from this spot. Sara would make a small stand of her own. Nobody at school wanted to join her. They all thought she was weird. She knew that she was, but that didn't bother her. She wore her silver trainers, crystal necklace, and fairy hairpins with pride. She would find her tribe at uni.

Sara was going to study environmental sciences at university. Then she was going to campaign or join a campaign; she was going to do *something* to reverse the damage wrought by humanity on their precious planet. Her parents said they were proud that she was going to be a scientist to her face. She knew, however, that they wished she had gone into medicine.

She had planned to do that until she started watching climate centred documentaries. Sara was horrified at what they showed her. She felt sick at the thought that she was a part of the problem. How many pints of milk had she consumed? How many burgers had she bought and not even finished?

As she sat berating herself, a woman had perched on the bench next to her. She was wearing a hi-vis jacket and carried a binbag and litter pick. Sara looked back to river and saw that much of the debris, that had so upset her when she first arrived, was gone. She turned her attention back to the woman who smiled at her warmly.

'You're right,' said the woman, her voice was bright as birdsong. 'You too can do *something* to reverse the damage.' She then got up and walked off along the river path.

Sara noticed that the back of her hi-vis was stamped with the picture of a fairy tied in barbed wire.

Inspired, Sara got up and followed her. As she walked behind the woman, Sara realised that she could help with cleaning up the river. She would start her *something* today.

The Original Suffolk Changeling Folktale
Retold by Hannah King

In the 1190s, around thirty years after the Wildman of Orford had been chained in a castle on the Suffolk coast, the manor was home to a family, servants and a fairy child. At first, they believed that a spirit was haunting the manor and called for an exorcist, but the servants had grown fond of him and asked the family to let him stay. The family agreed.

The fairy boy claimed he was a changeling, a human child who had been born in Lavenham and had been stolen by Ferishers (fairy folk) and that he could not come back in human form until seven years were up. The Ferishers allowed him to come to the human world but he had to wear a hat that made him invisible. Only once did he remove it and appeared to the family as a very small child dressed in white.

After seven years, he disappeared from the manor, and rumour has it that one of the children later saw a young boy with his mother, a boy who looked just like the fairy boy.

The Changeling That Didn't Want to Come Back

The day that this place first became significant to her; the sky was overcast. The rain made little pitter-patters on the hood of the red raincoat she was wearing, borrowed from the back of the blue 1957 Chevrolet Bel Air convertible. They hadn't planned to come to the Shotley Marshes. It was getting late. Everything was bathed in a warm evening glow. Her previously perfectly ironed yellow dress snagged on the thorns of a hawthorn bush. Ma would kill her later, she thought, as they made their way swiftly along the shingle path, her hand in his, and her little brown boots getting covered in the marsh mud.

She'd loved growing up in Suffolk. Always a moment away from playing in the countryside, throwing sticks at her brothers and climbing trees; coming home covered in the mud and being rushed straight up to the bathroom to get rid of the smell, something close to rotten eggs. But they lived close enough to Ipswich that she could secure her hair with bobby pins, put on her best dress, and spend a night drinking too much Tom Collins and dancing till her feet hurt.

It was strange to be back, especially alone.

She walked for a good while until she found the gap in the hedge, remembering how he'd laughed and pulled the leaves out of her hair. This had been what he wanted to show her; If she turned her head to the left, she could see the muddy river Orwell, if she turned it to the right, she could see golden fields stretching for miles. Two typical Suffolk scenes meeting in one spot 'for those days when you can't decide where to go'.

Once, sitting side by side, he had told her the story of Malekin, a changeling from Suffolk back in 1100. As he'd explained how the ferishers switched the children for fourteen years, his eyes went dark and he stared off into the distance.

'At fourteen years of age, that is when the human can return.'

'Are they happy to return?' she'd asked, and he'd told her that some of them are, not all of them. At this moment, a deep sadness came into his eyes and desperate to bring some relief she told him about the fairies of Stowmarket, where her mother had lived, small little creatures that mostly stayed underground and were very secretive.

He didn't look at her the whole time, but she knew he was listening by the way he narrowed his eyes thoughtfully. They then got into a deep discussion about secret tunnels underneath Suffolk, and all the ones they had heard of. To hear him speak, you'd have thought he'd seen them with his own eyes.

Turning to her with urgency he told her, 'I'll come back. I'll meet you right here, this spot. In seven years. But this is the last time I'm coming to Shotley until then.'

In the months that followed, he grew increasingly distant. He was no longer interested in the Shotley Marshes and instead they would go together to a place called Woolpit where apparently some green children had emerged from a secret tunnel. He would be distracted as they walked, and she was beginning to understand that she had lost him. If she ever really had him in the first place.

The last trip they ever took was to where he claimed were some old castle ditches. With excitement he told her how this was probably where the child was taken in the Malekin folk story, which meant somewhere around here would be the tunnel they used.

Already feeling a foreboding sense of sorrow, she followed behind, keeping her eyes on her muddy boots instead of the views around them, although she did pause to look at the little church.

After what felt like hours, they came across an old moat with brambles and nettles everywhere. She wasn't interested in having her legs torn to shreds, so she told him to go ahead and that she would wait for him. She waited until dark, but he never came back.

And now she was back in Shotley, seven years later, in the spot he had shown her. If she turned her head to the left, she could see the muddy river Orwell, if she turned it to the right, she could see golden fields stretching for miles.

She stood and watched the clouds go by, her dress blowing in the wind beneath her raincoat. As the overcast sky started to go pink and dim, she thought about giving up.

And then she heard the snap of a twig.

The Original Battle of Bloodmoor Hill, Folktale of Gisleham circa 500 AD by Jeremy Evans

Ghosts haunt the land where the bloody battle of Bloodmoor Hill stands. The Roman Britons were viciously slain by a horde of marauding Anglo-Saxons. It is said that a man, making his way home across the hill one foggy night several years ago now, heard the cries of a bloody siege and the metallic clash of blades. It was as if the very battle itself was retold to him in a moment of terror.

The truth of slaughter has been lost to the mists of time. But sleep you not late into the morning, in case you too lie in bed and find your throat slit by an enemy.

Live well, because the slaughter may be tomorrow.

The Tale of the Slaughter on the Hill

Up on the very top of the grassy hill, where the wind flutes in pretty eddies and the grass mixes with wildflowers, a beautiful woman watches a small child running towards her. She opens her arms to the child and smiles. But then, just as the child comes near, a heavy fog swirls and turns and falls, the day darkens to night and the child is gone. The beautiful woman and the grassy hill are gone into the fog, into memory.

I remember the week it happened very well. It was the second week in March 2020. I was expecting to see my granddaughter again. And my daughter, and my great-grand-daughter all at once. My birthday treat in the care home. I was quite the excited one. Ninety-one years old and giddy with joy. My great-grand-daughter at just a few months over five years old had a steadier head than mine. My Bert always said I was lively, given to excitement and he loved me for it.

I was married to Bert for seventy years. Almost seventy. He died just a week before our wedding anniversary. Our platinum anniversary. We were married the same year as Queen Elizabeth and Prince Phillip. 1947 – 2017.

The care home had a lovely garden, the spring sunshine was beautiful: warm, bright, and endless. I sat out in the garden, enjoying the sound of playful blackbirds.

The care home had a good reputation too, and when I fell ill with pneumonia last year, it seemed sensible to find somewhere where they could look after me.

After Bert went, I became quite forgetful. One of the things I forgot to do was to eat, so I got as thin as a pin. I will admit to the mirror that I'm not quite as young as I once was. There was the time I forget about the boiled eggs. That's what decided my daughter. Apparently, I nearly burned the house down, according to her.

Maybe I did and maybe I didn't.

I wanted to go into sheltered accommodation where you live quite independently, but she persuaded me a care home was better.

I was sitting there in the garden, waiting for my girls to visit when the young lady who cares for me started walking across garden towards me. I knew something was up. Serenity she was called. I always loved her name. It suited her well. She had long, flowing hair and a pretty, round face. Coming across the grass though, for some reason she looked very troubled.

'I am so sorry,' she said, and I knew it. They weren't coming. I began to cry. To see my great-grand-daughter, would have been such a joy.

Serenity began to cry too then.

'They're not allowed to come. Nobody is.'

And that was how the Coronavirus – such is its status that the world knows its name – stole my birthday from me. My last birthday.

The next day, the care home felt solemn, it was as if a ghost had slipped through the building in the night. Two of our elderly ladies – I called them elderly; they were ninety-six and ninety-eight – had died in the night. Even the weather had changed. There was terrible thick fog outside. One of the men here with dementia was moaning and wailing through the building. Calling out the names of the two ladies, as if he was the town crier and he had been charged with mourning their deaths. All day we had to listen to him hearing him coming down the hall, arms flailing in the air, moaning and moaning.

Serenity called me by phone personally that evening. Very sweet of her. She couldn't come in to work, you see. She had to stay away. She was ill. So was her friend, the girl who works on the other side of the hall. And the young man who worked with the men. He was ill too.

A few days later, things were worse. We all knew what it was about. A deadly virus attacking the world. I'd lived through many difficult times. I was a child in the Blitz, but March was the saddest month of my life.

All that week, my daughter phoned me every morning and evening. She was scared. I comforted her as best I could. By the end of the week, another three of the residents had been taken ill. By then, I was hot and suffering from a ticklish cough. And the funny thing was I lost my sense of taste. I may have been getting forgetful, but I wasn't a silly old woman, thank you! And by then, I knew I had the virus.

That was when my granddaughter Judith, set up a Facetime call so I could see and talk to my great-grand-daughter, Sophie. That was a joy.

Sophie told me to think of the future and not to worry about a thing. She showed me Bear-boo, her favourite toy. She said he was sending a big hug. She squeezed him to show me.

Then they sent me a 'virtual' hug. I pretended to hug them back. When the call was finished, I wept to myself. I knew it would be the last time we spoke, you see.

The Coronavirus had come for me. I was not afraid. You

see, certainty was not as frightening as uncertainty. Knowing it was time took almost all the weight of fear from my shoulders. Just let it be quick, I told myself.

I became a ghost in the dew. A young woman, fresh-faced and beautiful, for every young girl is beautiful. I walked the grassy hill so pretty with wildflowers. Sometimes I was a fairy barefooted in my prettiest dress, looking for my Bert.

My grandchildren and great-grandchildren in the mist of future time, heard my soft singing, and the music of my happy life. As the fog comes down on the hill, I see her again, and I want to ask her, Sophie, you will remember me, won't you?

The Original Faines of Hethersett Folktale
Retold by Kay Saberton

The Faines are said to be large animals the size of cows. With their enormous glowing saucer-like eyes, they haunt the village of Hethersett at night. Nobody quite knows what these terrifying creatures look like, but there are many tales of the beasts. Each storyteller has had their own version, and here is mine.

Our story begins with a man who was walking home late one night. On his journey, he spotted the outline of a large unidentifiable shape in front of him. His heart skipped a beat. Could it be a large, abandoned dog? A lost cow perhaps?

Slowly, the creature turned around. Revealing its gigantic luminous eyes that bore into the man's face. Terrified, he quickly spun around and ran in the opposite direction. Fearful of what this enormous shadow might be.

But he found that the creature matched his pace and would not allow him to escape his burning sight. If the man sped up or slowed down, the creature remained there right next to him. Absolutely horrified, the man hid behind a building hoping to evade the creature.

When he peered out, he found that the creature was still there, waiting for him. The large glowing eyes staring at him from a distance. The man squatted behind the derelict building for what felt like an eternity. Eventually, after peeking around the building many times, he looked to find that the creature had miraculously vanished. Such was the man's curiosity that he began looking for the beast, not believing what he'd seen. Where could it have gone, he wondered? The man retraced his steps back to where he'd first noticed the creature standing still in the middle of the road. But it was no longer there.

It is said that despite their huge size and fierce reputation, the Faines always leave their victims alive. Nobody knows if these creatures are real or ghostly apparitions; yet everyone who has sighted one reports of the terror they felt. Having heard a tale of the Faines, people have often visited the village of Hethersett, desperate to catch a glimpse of the creatures. Some say that the Faines are protective creatures that appear to lone travellers, escorting them on their journey. If this is to be true, maybe there is more to the Faines than first meets the eye.

The Barfly Bumpkin

There's a man in this pub who seems to have been here all day, drinking whatever his troubles are away. He has several empty pint glasses stacked in front of him, the foam lingering on each rim. I watch the staff giving the bloke occasional sideways glances as they serve other patrons. I'm several tables over, but I can hear him muttering to himself and occasionally letting out a muffled barking sound. He's obviously a local, no pub I've ever been in would ever tolerate a fella like that. It's like there's an invisible barrier around him that prevents anyone from interacting with him. I am intrigued in him despite myself. He can't be happy, that much is certain.

Suddenly, his vacant, red eyes catch mine. We stare at each other. A Mexican standoff in a small village pub. Well, there's only one thing I can do now I've been spotted. I hop down from my bar stool and make my way across the sticky floor.

On my short journey over I wonder, what am I gonna say? I could offer to buy him a drink, but he looks like he's had enough already if I'm honest.

'Hey, sorry if you thought I was staring. I was just wondering if you're alright mate?'

He looks disinterested, no longer looking at me. His blank unfocused eyes are darting about the place. Those eyes are frantic, furiously searching, busy with the thirst for knowledge. Betraying the busy mind within. He whimpers softly. Clearly, something is bothering this guy. I reach out and place a hand on his shoulder to comfort him, to get his attention. He jerks his body away the moment my hand makes impact.

'Excuse me, what do ye think you're doin'?' he shouts. The rest of the pub stop and look over at us. I'm a little flustered. I don't know what to say.

'I-I'm sorry,' I stammer. 'I didn't mean to startle you. I was just asking if you're alright?'

He looks me up and down.

'Why do ye care, huh? I'm just some fella in a pub. Why don't ye ignore me like the rest?' He pauses. 'They fink I'm a joke,' he mutters.

'I'm just a person who cares, is all. I'll leave you be if you'd prefer, I just thought you might wanna talk?'

He assesses me again. Weighing up if I'm worth trusting. After taking a large sip of his beer, the froth framing his mouth, he nods at the stool next to him.

'Okay, okay, I'll chat to ye. No-one else bloody wants to, do they? I wasn't always the village nutter, you know.'

'No?'

He sighs and drags his hand across his face, catching the beer foam on his lip. He looks deeply into my eyes.

'I was walkin' home late from the pub one night. Made it all the way back to the new estate. Well, I was only ten minutes or so from my house when I saw this shadow. It scared the life outta me. Never seen anythin' like it! So, I walk on, a little bit quicker. But when I turned around it was there. A beast, with huge glowing eyes. Thought it was a cow at first. But it was something different. Something weird. I damn near had a heart attack. I ran home without looking back and locked the door behind me. Next day, I told the lads what I'd seen, and they just laughed at me. Thought I'd had too much to drink and made it up. I know what I saw, and I can't seem to forget it.'

Upon finishing his tale, he picks up his pint with shaking hands. Something had happened, that much was clear. But a cow with glowing eyes? He was off his nut. We chatted for a little while longer, mostly out of politeness on my part, before parting ways.

I'd just moved to the village. I didn't know the area well yet, so I drift in the direction I hope will lead me home. I can't stop thinking about that story. A cow, with glowing eyes. Couldn't be real, surely? He must have been so drunk that he hallucinated it.

But then I see something moving in the corner of my eye. A shadow moving rapidly towards me in the distance. It couldn't be, could it? It must be the trick of the light, a cat in a bush. I shouldn't look back. My curiosity gets the better of me and I turn around to find myself staring into a pair of glowing eyes. I freeze. My blood running cold. He was right. The drunk man was right. I trip over the curb and fall over into the road. The glowing eyes and enormous shadow approach me. It towers above me and I recoil in fear. This is it. The end. I close my eyes waiting for something to happen. Nothing comes.

A quiet 'moooooo' finds its way through the darkness. Then, roaring laughter. The lights are dimmed and what I perceived as a shadow, is removed. It's the man from the pub. And he's laughing in my face.

'That's what ye get for judgin' strangers! An' they say I'm the nutter. You dumb city folk movin' out 'ere, don't know nothin', so easy to mess with.'

I stare at him in disbelief.

Still laughing, he says 'Welcome to Hethersett.'

The Original Eva of Dunwich Folktale
Retold by Muriel Moore-Smith

Once, many years ago, when Dunwich was a bustling port and not the tiny hamlet it is today, a young maiden, Eva, was out walking along its harbour walls. In the distance, she spied a ship with magnificent sails, quite possibly the largest and most impressive ship she had ever seen. Curious, she hurried towards the place where the ship was moored.

When she arrived, she saw that the ship was not quite as large and magnificent as she had at first thought. However, securing the ropes of the vessel was a young sailor. He was so smart in his colourful clothes made of exotic silks that Eva thought he was the most alluring man she had ever seen. He looked up from his task and saw Eva, with her rust-coloured hair plaited down her strong back and her cream dress tipped with black. He told her she was beautiful, a child of nature. He said that if she met with him that evening, he would bring her riches the like of which she had never seen.

Eva agreed, enchanted by this exotic stranger who had arrived so unexpectedly on the shores of her town.

Later that evening, when Eva met the sailor as arranged, his hands were empty of gifts. Instead, he forced himself upon the young girl. He half-crushed her and tore her cream dress, tangled her rust-coloured hair. When it was over, the sailor left her on the beach.

In the morning, when Eva awoke from the stupor of

sleep, she found the sailor gone. Arising from her sandy bed, she saw on the horizon the sailor's ship, now an insignificant speck. She looked down at her torn dress, her tangled hair. In an anguish of sorrow for all she had lost, she reached down inside her dress, and ripped out her heart, throwing it towards the vanishing ship.

Today, if you walk along Dunwich beach, in amongst the pebbles and wood and pieces of brick, you might find a wooden heart. However much you look, don't pick it up; its sorrow may become your sorrow.

The Wooden Heart

Evan leans his back against one of the concrete tank's defenses. He looks south, down the beach at the trucks and diggers and cranes which are finally still and silent. Behind them, like an alien craft dropped into the soft lines between sand and sky, glows Sizewell B. Its monstrous reactor sits on top of the sharp lines of its rectangular base.

He swears, even at this distance, that he can feel it pulsing, emitting waves of energy whilst it pours its warm, contaminated waste into the sea. He is still in disbelief that the building work has started on yet another reactor. Evan remembers the heart-felt protests, the letters written, petitions signed, all crushed to nothing because of the whim of a transient government. He isn't sure why he is surprised. He knows the mantra has been instant solutions over long-term sustainability for so long. He knows how easily people are enticed by money. He imagines some Fat Cat, exchanging this sleepy stretch of the Suffolk coast for an exotic island in the Indian Ocean. The trouble is, Evan knows, we will all pay the price in the end, even the Fat Cat on his island.

Evan makes his way slowly back down the path towards the reserve. After the ghastly white of the reactor and its gaudy side show of trucks and cars, the reed beds seem to him to reveal all the magnificent subtlety of nature's palette. Every day, around this time, he marvels at the way the reeds seem to absorb light, only now, in the soft approach of evening, to give it back to the world. All is amber, ochre, soft blue. Evan knows that this is the way of nature: whatever is taken is always given back.

Somewhere in the distance, Evan distinguishes a mewling cry which punctuates the air like a question. The hairs on Evan's arms stand up, a mother responding to a baby's cry. He scrambles to the edge of the reed bed and crouches down, looking up into the fading light of the evening sky. There, just above the reed bed, two birds are performing an aeronautical display of astonishing grace and majesty. One, almost black, its vast wings stretching up towards the sky in a low v, flies low across the golden reeds. The other, smaller with a breast the colour of clay, is in pursuit. It stops, seemingly mid-flight, and circles underneath. It is as if the dance has been choreographed and yet, sitting there, Evan can think of no earthly mortal capable of this ballet.

He feels a lump in his throat. Here they are, the Marsh Harriers, returned to Minsmere to breed. *Circus aeruginosus*. Circles of rust. Evan is not quite sure if he has translated it correctly, but he feels that the ancients have captured it correctly. They are circles of rust, swooping up there in the Suffolk sky, a reminder of the regeneration of nature, its faithfulness.

They are the beating heart of this place, thinks Evan. They are what makes all the hard work, the early mornings, worthwhile. They are the beating heart of Minsmere. Some-where, deep inside, he wonders if they might be his beating heart.

The light at Minsmere is different in the mornings. Harder, cooler. Instead of warm ochres and ambers, the reeds look yellow and brown. Evan can barely discern any bird song over the noise of the diggers, the hauling of hydraulics, the shouts of workmen. As he heads towards the beach to check for debris washed up overnight, he hears the shrill cry of a kittiwake.

Lying across the beach is a large length of bright blue net fencing, strewn out along the grey pebbles like an exotic jelly fish. It is impossible to miss. Evan knows what he will find, bound up in its web: a black backed gull or perhaps a tern.

Evan stands over the tangled plait of plastic and searches along its length. At the very end he spots the yellow of a hooked beak just visible through the blue plastic. Evan's heart races. Not a gull or tern then. He kneels down and starts to unfurl the plastic. When he has finished, Evan sits and examines what is in front of him. The long black body, the vast black wings ending in curled feathers, the white hood. It is the female Marsh Harrier. She had been gathering sticks for her nest on the stones. There are still a few twigs in her beak.

He picks her up. He is astonished by how heavy she is. One wing droops, lifeless, next to her body. It is so long that it almost touches Evan's feet. It will never soar the skies again. Evan finds that he has started to run, the hawk carried in front of him like an offering. He runs up the beach, heedless of the pebbles which usually make his progress difficult. He heads into the reserve and towards the wood store. He knows what he must do.

When he comes out, he has exchanged the body of the bird for an axe. He is a man of the land, and the axe swings confidently by his side, its blade shining in the early morning sun. He makes his way along the beach, towards the power station. The journey does not take him long.

If you visit Minsmere today, sitting on the edge of the beach between Dunwich and Sizewell, you will see a sculpture of a large bird, fashioned lovingly in oak. The inscription beneath reads *Circus aeruginosus, Female Marsh Harrier.* However much you look, do not touch it; its sorrow may become your sorrow.

Student New Angle Writing Awards Shortlisted and Winning entries 2021
Winner 2021 Bradley Garnham

For this story, I chose to focus on the history of the old town of Dunwich, just north of Sizewell, that was progressively washed into the sea by storms in the 13th and 14th Centuries. There is an enduring ghost story surrounding the loss of the town, and people say that you can sometimes hear the bells of the ruined churches across the sea. While I certainly dramatized it a bit, my story itself was entirely true – I did hear the bells at Dunwich many years ago, when I was walking with my Grandma along the shore.

The Singing Tides

My grandmother once led me along a winding coastal path, one windy winter's morning many years ago. There was a cold and quiet mist about us as we trudged along the beach, accompanied by a biting wind which nipped our necks and hands. I watched in quiet envy as her dog bounced across the surf and shore, oblivious to the chill which had me burrowed in my coat. Perhaps through spite or boredom, as we shuffled on our way, I occasionally grabbed a rock or stone and tossed it into the water, listening as it splashed into the frigid sea. I was unaware of what this broken coast had lost already. Unaware that murky waters sometimes throw things back.

I didn't notice it at first, in fact I hardly noticed it at all. A soft and subtle song that rose up from the depths, sailing inwards with the waves and onwards past the hills, before it faded gently into the marshy fields beyond. The tune was faint and distant, like the memory of a memory. Some dark and ancient sound that had long since been forgot. A chorus of discordant bells, unlike anything I'd heard before, who sang with many voices, some who whispered, some who roared. It froze me in an instant and forced my gaze towards the water, staring out into the haze to find its unseen source. The mists began to thicken as their ghostly chiming grew. Bong… tolled the bells, rising quickly from the sea. Bong… they came again, growing louder than before. Bong… those voices cried, from their graves beneath the shore.

I felt the world grow cold and dim, as shadows smothered light, guided by the music to some dark and wretched place. A torrent thundered from above as the waves began to roil, jagged bolts of lightning giving form to the figures in the gloom. Suddenly there stood a town, where nothing stood before, laid bare beneath the rolling storm and helpless in its wake. The bells were screaming through the night, as people fled their homes, only to be caught and dragged into the raging sea. I watched as houses splintered and as mighty buildings fell, as towers built to honour god were taken in His wrath. This is what they sang of, this calamity that came. Of the greed and hunger of this beast that swallowed everything it found; their memories of all they'd lost, and would never see again.

I felt my grandma tug my hand, and I snapped back to her side, awoken from a trance I never noticed I was in.

I never spoke of what I heard, or thought I had that day. Even now it frightens me to wonder what it was. Because I know that I heard something, on that quiet, forlorn shore. Some sad, forgotten music, made by sad, forgotten things. The distant chime of ancient bells, that called out from the depths. A mournful dirge for those long past, who'll ring them nevermore.

SNAP Writing Awards 2021 Runner Up, Sarah Clark

I already knew that I wanted to set this story in and around the Fens, and that it was going to be witchcraft related. I came up with the idea of Agamede, a young pregnant village girl, terrified and looking for the witch to help her out of her predicament, as the starting point. I researched character names, herbs, the plants that would have been growing on the Fens at the time and the wildlife that would have been around, even down to the pike that Aelfthryth was fishing for when Agamede first meets her. I tried to make it as geographically and historically accurate as I could. It helped that I could already picture Wicken Fen as it is in the 21st century – I tried to imagine how eerie it would have looked and felt 1000 years or more earlier and my imagination took me from there.

Aelfthryth

The never-ending, darkening sky that stretched Wicken Fen into sunset brought with it the promise of another cold autumnal night. The rooks were beginning to quieten, the harvest mice scurried back to their nests and the scent of ripening onions filled the air. A murmuration of starlings dived and curled above, heading towards the reedbeds.

There was no soul about, except Agamede.

Agamede crept quietly through the long grass, looking around her anxiously as she headed towards Monk's Lode. She carried with her a basket in which she was concealing her salvation. Small bundles of Herb of Grace and Pennyroyal and a handful of ripe Juniper berries were concealed underneath a selection of autumn fruits; ripe plums, sweet apples and plump blackberries. She could not be seen here. She looked around, warily, crunching the long grass and feeling the give of the marshy ground as she trod.

She felt her belly. It was beginning to swell and if anyone had stared at her for too long they would be able to see the outline of her shame against the material of her dress. She did not have long. It had taken her weeks of visiting the Fen at dusk to find Aelfthryth.

Agamede had been warned about Aelfthryth ever since she had been very young. She was not to be trusted; she lived alone on the Fen, was at least 200 years of age and spoke regularly with the Devil. Aelfthryth was barren, and it was said that if she came upon a woman with child, she could bring on her courses just by looking at her. Agamede had been afraid of Aelfthryth's fearsome reputation, but the first time she saw her sitting by the Lode, fishing for pike, she was not afraid of her at all. Aelfthryth was but a tiny, kindly woman with grey-brown hair that reached to her shoulders. She smelled of lavender and mugwort. She spoke softly, and only spoke as much as she needed to.

Agamede saw movement by the ash thicket set back from the water's edge, changed direction and picked up speed to walk in the direction of the trees. The sun had dropped fully beyond the horizon, and the once-benign Fen landscape became a hiding place for the demons and monsters in Agamede's imagination. Her heart began to pound, and she could have sworn that she felt the child quickening. No, she thought, it cannot be, I cannot be so far progressed.

She reached the thicket. There was no sign of Aelfthryth. The trees groaned in the breeze. There was a scent of lavender; Aelfthryth had been here. Agamede felt the quickening sensation again, then was gripped by a pain so intense that she gasped and fell to the ground. The fruit scattered as Agamede groaned. She lay under the trees until the pain subsided and then, made her way home.

Aelfthryth watched her from the shadows, smiling as she stroked her pregnant belly.

Shortlisted Stories and Poems

Framlingham Castle by Amy Bessent

Panic atomised us as we ran
Backs against the sun
abandoning the blossoms,
we went home
and stayed there for a while.
Hidden from the eyes of Time,
who peeps
through the arrow-slits
and whose embrasures
swallow us whole

A short walk
but worlds away -
absence intensifies the longing
dilutes memories,
and coaxes them into dust
so that
like bricks,
they might be replaced,
recomposed in newness
and crumbling Tudor redness

Set them in the stone
and keep them in your walls
until we may walk atop them once more
among the crenellations
the palisades
and the parapets;
treading the phantom walkways,
the earth tones and the umber
set against ghosts of lyres and lutes
now out of tune

I long for nervous heights
to muse
upon the nettles
which gather on green meadows
the way cow-parsley sprawls from the umbel;
reaching upwards,
rising through the tangled undergrowth,
from the dungeon to the dreaming-tower
as we unfurl,
renewed

The Afternoon Walk by Jeremy Evans

Deep, thick furrowed earth like chocolate. New shoots of winter wheat glistening in low sunlight. This is Suffolk. Fields up and down, hazed sky as blue as Turkish waters.

Our boots are heavy with clay. Rusty the Labrador hunts, sniffs, stops and snuffles.

A pheasant cries and flies – all flapping wings and bluster.

Rusty's tail wags happily. Satisfied that the pheasant has been rudely outed, he follows a different scent.

A scattering of trees. A see-through hedge. A raptor on a telephone pole, secretive calmness in the sky, she follows our progress.

A car on a road – an annoying addition – finally fades into the distance.

The sea now. Grey and muddy – I know it to be so, so shallow. Calm and flat, a lazy drift southward. White-gold reflections stab my eye.

I stop to take it in and snap pictures on my phone.

Further on is the pub. There will be a fire and an Adnams. If we're allowed in, what with lockdown, we'll finish there.

A horse in a field comes to nuzzle. It snorts and shakes its head. Steam rises. I put out a hand to stroke his nose, but he shies his head away.

My wife answers an urgent message – email, text or WhatsApp, I'm not sure.

I pass through a kissing gate and the dog gets stuck and is told off.

'Haven't you learned how these work, yet?'

He slinks like Fagin and soon forgets.

Our hands are cold, but even so my wife is restored.

The sun is getting lower.

A line of wispy cloud is building, and it has captured the sun's heat.

I can see the pub. And, sprayed with mud, our car.

And I can imagine thirstily the pint that's calling.

The light has dulled. Purple cloud passes the late sun. Long shadows form, intense yellow burns softly on the chocolate earth. I am in danger of beauty.

Dog on the lead.

'You first.'

Inside it's warm, and bright electric light recalibrates my eye.

Inside, it brings the walk to an end.

A Good Day's Work in Lavenham by Amber Spalding

Mary tied her shoelaces, *through the loop and into the castle* – the way her mother had taught her. She picked up the singular key hanging by the door, and felt the wind twirl round her skirt as she made her way to work.

Growing up in a remote village called Shimpling, Mary was the daughter of William - a livestock farmer, and Elizabeth, a former seamstress. At the age of eighteen, she had acquired all of the skills needed to set upon her own life in the neighbouring village, Lavenham – a wealthy town, renowned for its wool trade. Mary had travelled by horse to a family friend, John, who offered her a small attic bedroom in his thatched house, on the agreement that Mary made his winter clothes.

The Market Square was warmed by the morning sunlight. The smell of bread lingered through the air as Mary walked past the bakery, her senses intertwined. It was intoxicating, her stomach rumbled at the thought of consuming it. Following the scent like an animal, Mary made her way to the Guildhall, ready for work. Dormant butterflies started to flutter in her veins as she allowed herself to get excited. Her whole life stretched out ahead of her like a perpetual rainbow.

A small man appeared in the doorway; his body was covered in a crisp dirt that stained, head to toe. He wore wooden-soled sandals with leather straps which stuck to the floor like a magnet. In a rich Suffolk accent, Mary was instructed to walk around back where a gentleman called Thomas would show her the ropes. A unanimous *baa* greeted her on arrival; it was a sound she remembered from her childhood. Thomas was a tall, stern man, who rather than spoke, grunted and pointed to what he wanted. At first, he was difficult to understand, but Mary soon deciphered his code, *Aigh* meant she was doing something right. By five o'clock, the duo had sheared almost fifty of Suffolk's finest sheep and bagged up the wool to be distributed. Thomas said that his wool had been sent to Russia last month and in return, paid him a wealthy sum. With this, he bought enough grains to last him until spring.

'You've got yourself a job,' the small man said as Mary left the Guildhall.

'Wednesday week we've got a large shipment off to Essex, so you better shear those sheep until there's wool coming out of your ears!'

Mary walked home with a spring in her step. The market had closed for the day and the distant sound of civilization hummed in the night. With her new home in sight, she rummaged for her key and found a large clump of wool – Mary kept it as a souvenir. As she turned the key right, John was sitting in front of the roaring fire, rubbing his hands together for warmth.

'Good evening Mary,' he said. 'A good day's work?'

Christchurch Reminiscence by Elliot Woods

I'm beginning to become reminiscent. Sentimental about simple things. Thinking I've taken places for granted. Like the park. Not in the sense I had as a child when I'd go there to play and always whine about having to leave, no, never that again. The sense that it's a lovely place to get lost. Either following the paths or wandering across the greens it always felt like there was something off in the distance when I was younger. Going there during it all it was like an expanse I had never explored before. Past all the hills were twisting roads blanketed with foliage that intersected like a web. You can loop back around and take a different way every time to feel pleasantly active.

At the top of the hill is that playground I mentioned and played in. It changed a lot over the years. The one thing that did, I think. The rest is the same; the steep hill I ran down and hurt myself on, the chairs, the buildings. Perhaps the trees remaining untouched helps keep this comforting familiarity. Preserving simplistic childhood memories.

It's fitting the statues are there then. You cannot miss them. Two small spires and a sun all atop plaques. I never read them. I don't think most people would. But they're still standing and might even outlive me. Forever paying homage to the soldiers and martyrs. I feel like I should read what they say when it's all over, since we'll also probably fall to being ignored in the future.

In the middle is the manor, it's unmissable. There's a garden outside of it that is quite lovely as I recall, though that's for all we recall. I remember touring that giant house of history and recreation with the constant want of moving on. It was quite impressive though. Probably still is. Fitting that it's the figurehead of a place that retains so much similarity.

I can recall playing in the park. That time I fell and grazed my knee badly. The long walks I would take snaking in between the greenery and seeing all I could because I couldn't do much else in this time. Despite all the good and bad it's still a fond place, something that I can remember and revisit without fear of change. A constant in a time of turbulence. That's all we need, sometimes. Nothing grand, or mind-blowing, or perhaps even that interesting. Something ever-present amongst the change. Mine is a park I still like to walk in.

Notes on the writers

Amy Bessant

Amy Bessant graduated with an undergraduate degree in English from the University of Suffolk in 2018 and returned in 2020 to begin the MA in Creative and Critical Writing. Her interests are critical theory and subjectivity, with a particular emphasis on the relationship between the unconscious and technology.

The reason that the tale of the Rendlesham Mermaid was chosen is to do with how little is known about it, and one of the most interesting things about folktales is how they are preserved across time. What is also very intriguing about the tale is the theme of water and the sometimes ominous things it can hide. Water offers an interesting place in which to write themes of desire and prohibition which are common to many folktales, so it was important to retain these elements in the retelling.

Amber Spalding

Amber Spalding is currently a third-year English student at the University of Suffolk. She loves to read and write, with particular interests in speculative fiction, historical writing, and representations of nature in literature. As a newbie to the writing world, she has been experimenting with poetry and short story writing, looking at the entanglements between human consciousness and the environment. One of her favourite poems, 'Homesick' was published in January 2021 and has just recently featured in two poetry anthologies. Outside of her studies, you will usually find Amber reading, travelling or in the countryside taking sunset pictures. After University, she seeks to continue her studies in literature, exploring how socio-political factors influence the literary canon.

Her reimagined folktale is based upon the local legend 'The Devil at Westleton Church'. When researching Suffolk folktales, Amber was adamant that she wanted to write something ghastly and terrifying. Sifting through various newspaper articles, she came across Devilish sightings at St. Peter's Church. Inspired by her love of Gothic literature, Amber decided to rewrite the tale through a 21st century lens, focusing on a group of teenagers who recreate the ritual to summon the Devil. Also, with a love for nature, Amber wanted to focus heavily on the narrator's surroundings and explore this transition between day and night, whilst also creating a horror story

Alison Dudeney

Alison Dudeney is currently a student at the University of Suffolk on the MA course in Creative and Critical Writing. She lives in the wilds of Suffolk near to the coast where she has now found the opportunity and confidence to write full-time. Her writing focuses on nature, the uncanny, and the human psyche both in poetry and prose. As yet unpublished, she is currently working on a modern-day Gothic novel set in Suffolk.

Her folktale is called 'The Orwell Mermaid'. Alison chose this story because she is interested in the sea and mythical creatures. The Orwell mermaid wants to escape the sea because she is infatuated with a fisherman, in doing so she breaks a code which for her means death. The modern-day version centres on a trafficked girl and her attempt to escape. Hearing headlines about these kinds of stories, the focus is often on the perpetrators and one wonders about the victims' stories and to what lengths they go to escape the lives they are forced to live. Alison wanted to give a voice to these stories.

Caroline Roberts

Caroline Roberts is a writer and freelance theatre-maker based in Manningtree, which is almost in Suffolk. She is currently studying on the MA in Creative and Critical Writing at the University of Suffolk and pursuing her interest in female voices, especially mothers. As a mum herself, she is experiencing that time when a child moves into the teenage years; causing her to reflect on her role as a mother and the lives of the women in her own family history.

Caroline chose the story of 'Malekin' because although it tells of a bright spirit who delighted the family he visited; it doesn't acknowledge the potential grief of the family he has left behind. Having experienced loss herself, as so many people have, Caroline wanted to explore the transient nature of being a mother, and a parent. The fleeting moment, however long, when a child is with you, the impact is has emotionally, and the traces that remain.

Carol Love

Carol is currently a student at the University of Suffolk on the BA course in English Literature and Creative Writing. She was born in London but has lived most her life in Suffolk. After ten years working as a medical secretary, she realized her ambition and wanted to start writing her own words. As a mature student, she is currently rethinking everything she thought she knew about literature and learning new truths.

Her folktale is based on the Church at Akenham which has many rumours of strange happenings. There have been reports of the church bells ringing for no reason and a ghost has been sighted numerous times at its chapel window. However, it is most known for raising the Devil. A local legend which alleges that the Devil slumbers under a split gravestone and you risk his ire by running around the church thirteen times anticlockwise. Carol chose this story because of its longevity which is dependent on it being passed down from generation to generation. Carol brought a contemporary element to the folktale by basing it around a present-day friendship between two young boys who, she imagined, would be curious enough about the legend to go up and see the church. She brought it up-to-date by linking the ending with problems of homelessness and drug addiction which we see on our streets today.

Dinah Cowan

After early careers in corporate travel (which allowed her to indulge in her love of exploring the world) and primary education (which allowed her to indulge in long school holidays with her son and three stepdaughters), Dinah completed a BA (Hons) Education at Anglia Ruskin University in 2013, with the intention of progressing to teacher training. She began working, however, in professional services at ARU, before moving to a role at the University of Suffolk following relocation from Essex three years' ago. She is currently undertaking the MA in Creative and Critical Writing at the same institution, which has been invaluable in giving her the confidence and discipline she needed to indulge in her life-long desire to write. When not reading and writing, Dinah can be found gardening, indulging in artistic pursuits (with varying degree of success), or exploring Suffolk, by bicycle, with her partner.

Dinah chose The Stowmarket Fairies because she was charmed by the original tale of these raucous but benevolent intruders. She was drawn to this as a light-hearted folktale, feeling it leant to a more comedic reimagining than many of our traditional, cautionary tales. The notion that fairies may take over your housework and leave money on their departure – what a fabulous prospect!

Elliot Woods

Elliot Woods is a student on the MA course in Creative and Critical Writing at the University of Suffolk. He has lived in Suffolk his whole life. Elliot has maintained mainstream education despite facing the challenges of being on the Autistic Spectrum, and he continues to aspire to write professionally.

He chose the folktale of 'Spring-Heeled Jack' to adapt into 'King, Queen, Jack' purely for the interesting imagery of the character and the idea of a Suffolk bred nightmare creature which appealed to his own imagination. The reasoning behind the rewrite was to present what kind of monster Jack was conceived as; one that would target independent women in the 1900's. Elliot's modern version depicts Jack as representing society's stereotypical prejudice against single mothers and children with additional needs, he is supposed to be a monster after all.

Fiona Waters

Fiona Waters lives in Ipswich and is a current student on the MA Creative and Critical Writing course at the University of Suffolk, where she completed her undergraduate degree in English last year. Her study and writing interests include disability in fiction, the ethics of creative writing, and historical fiction.

Fiona wrote her modern-day folktale 'The Lost Shepherd' after being inspired by the sad legend of John Dobbs, whose gravestone in Kesgrave, Suffolk has been rumoured to be the cause of many strange occurrences throughout the last century. Fiona's folktale aims to explore the themes of grief, depression, and isolation through the eyes of a young twenty-first century man, Jack.

Hannah Daley

Hannah has been longlisted twice for the SNAP (Student New Angle Prize) and in 2018 she made the shortlist too. Hannah recently graduated with a first-class degree in BA (Hons) English from the University of Suffolk and is currently working towards her master's in Creative and Critical Writing at the same institution. When not researching for her course, Hannah can be found at Woodbridge Emporium, a small independent bookshop where she is training to be a bookseller, or at home with her toddler Lysander who keeps her very busy.

Hannah has a deep love of all things mythic and fairy tale, which she credits to her frequent trips to pantomimes as a small child with her family. When the opportunity arose to add to a contemporary folktale anthology, she could not pass it up. Hannah chose to revise 'Brother Mike', the story of a fairy who succumbs to death at the hands of human greed because she felt it spoke to contemporary environment concerns. From developing a cultural and critical awareness, Hannah finds herself drawn to eco-feminism and felt that this story would give her the chance to test this new passion.

Hannah King

The daughter of a keen sailor, Hannah grew up in Suffolk close to the marina. Hannah studied creative media and fine art before giving in to the pull of literature and creative writing and starting a degree at Suffolk University where her confidence in her writing took off. She hasn't stopped writing since.

Hannah has always loved faerie stories and used to leave cake for them under the tree in her garden. While she has relented that particular behaviour, she still can't resist a story about them. When considering which story to tell, it had to be about the faeries of Suffolk. Growing up, stories have been a safe place for Hannah and a refuge in difficult times. Reflecting on that, she wanted to capture the pull of this other world and the deep longing that can come when you're desperate to escape, just for a little while. And that was where the idea for a changeling craving to return to the magical world he'd once known came from.

Jeremy Evans

Jeremy Evans is married with two beautiful daughters. He is a keen sailor, and in his spare time, he writes novels, often with a sailing theme. He was longlisted for the Laxford Literary Prize in 2021 for his novel *Dubois of the Milice*.

Jeremy chose his folktale for the very fact that it is was incomplete. The battle of Gisleham occurred in around 500AD. There is no clear record of what happened, but it is understood that the Anglo-Saxons slaughtered Roman

Britons. The Roman Empire fell during this time and Britain became a different place, much changed. The myth of the Anglo-Saxons is strong in East Anglia. The folktale is brief, fractured, and the truth of what occurred is lost in the mist of time. Only the figurative (and possibly the real) ghosts of the story remain. Jeremy's modern folktale is about the spread of the Covid-19 virus through a care home. It is seen through the eyes of a resident who is kept separated from her family, and discovers she has the disease. On the face of it, marauding Anglo Saxons and the Coronavirus are not the same, but, of course, the parallels can be seen. Death, fear, and wholesale change are at the heart of both stories. Time is required to see the aftermath and the longer view of how Suffolk, Britain, and indeed the world are changed. After the virus, power shifts. There are those who are killed, those ruined but equally those who benefit and profit. The troubles continue long after the first great battle. The ghosts of this chaotic, invisible invasion will haunt us for many years to come. It is also possible that an unspoken Empire of social and health freedoms may have come to an end.

Kay Saberton

Kay Saberton is a writer and co-editor for Student Life Magazine, a regional award-winning charity and publication run for and by students. She currently lives in Norwich and her hobbies include painting, gaming, and taking her dogs for long walks. Kay achieved a first-class BA (Hons) English degree at the University of Suffolk and won several accolades, including the 2019 *East Anglian Daily Times Award* for Professional Writing, and the *Suffolk Book League Award* for the Best Dissertation in English. After immensely enjoying her dissertation project focused on Mary Shelley and her novel *Frankenstein*, Kay has returned to study on the MA in Creative and Critical Writing at the University of Suffolk where she is continuing to pursue her interest in Gothic literature, film studies, and Mary Shelley. At present, Kay is working on a novel about Fanny Wollstonecraft, a woman often overlooked in research of the Shelley-Godwin circle.

'The Faines of Hethersett' is a re-telling of a Norfolk folktale about the Faines, creatures with enormous glowing eyes. Kay chose this tale because she had recently moved and was interested to know if there were any local folktales in the area. She was fascinated to find that there was no established folktale about the Faines, only reported sightings from village locals. Her modern folktale, 'The Barfly Bumpkin,' plays on the idea of the local sighting as a man tells his story in a village pub. Kay wanted to subvert the often-serious tone of the folktale, instead writing something light-hearted. At the centre, the story is about how our initial judgments of people can be wrong, and that maybe there is more to people – and the Faines – than first meets the eye.

Muriel Moore-Smith

Muriel Moore-Smith has spent many years living in Suffolk, although she was born in The Netherlands and lived in sunny Southern California for three years. Muriel studied literature and music at various universities before becoming an English teacher and a semi-professional singer. Muriel no longer teaches but continues to sing and is studying part-time at the University of Suffolk for a Master of Arts degree in Creative and Critical Writing.

Muriel first heard the tale of Eva of Dunwich during a trip to The Hold, the new Suffolk Record's Office. The tale intrigued her because it evoked the fact that Dunwich was once a bustling port, a place where people who came from exotic locations might arrive. By a strange coincidence, on a recent visit to Dunwich, Muriel's daughter picked up a stone and said, 'It looks like a heart', which felt like confirmation that Eva's was the right story to tell. The updated version came from Muriel's love of that stretch of the Suffolk coastline, and the terrible way in which the continuing development of Sizewell threatens it. To her, as for many others, Minsmere itself has always seemed like such a haven, both for the many birds which congregate there and for the people who find solace at the sanctuary. Muriel wanted to emphasise that invading forces who promise much, have always come to this coastline. Sometimes what is lost in the process can never be replaced.